# Brighton Honeymoon

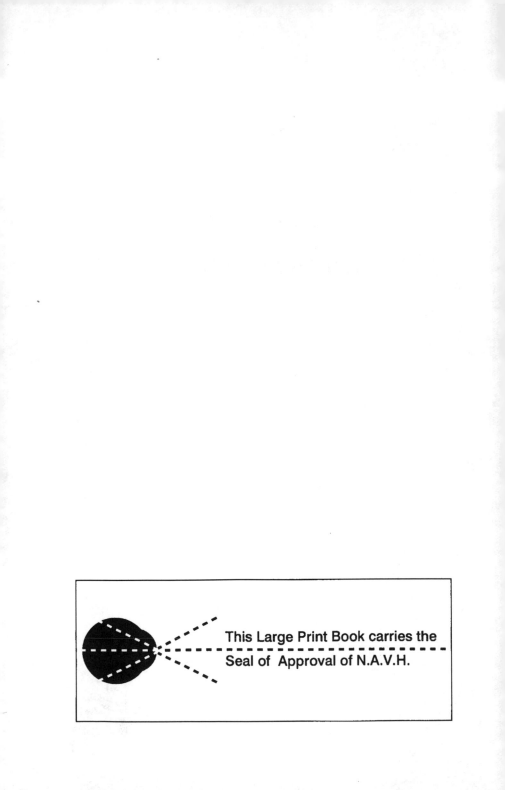

This Large Print Book carries the
Seal of Approval of N.A.V.H.

# Brighton
# Honeymoon

## Sheri Cobb South

**Thorndike Press** • **Waterville, Maine**

Published in 2002 by arrangement with
Prinny World Press.

Thorndike Press Large Print Romance Series.

The tree indicium is a trademark of Thorndike Press.

The text of this Large Print edition is unabridged.
Other aspects of the book may vary from the original edition.

Cover design by Deirdre Wait.

Set in 16 pt. Plantin by Myrna S. Raven.

Printed in the United States on permanent paper.

**Library of Congress Cataloging-in-Publication Data**

South, Sheri Cobb.
    Brighton honeymoon / Sheri Cobb South.
       p. cm.
    ISBN 0-7862-4273-6 (lg. print : hc : alk. paper)
    1. Large type books.   2. Impostors and imposture —
Fiction.   3. Brighton (England) — Fiction.   4. Nobility
— Fiction.   I. Title.
    PS3569.O755 B75 2002
    813'.54—dc21                                    2002190356

To all those who asked for
"more about Mr. Brundy."

# 1

You may tempt the upper classes
With your villainous demitasses,
But Heaven will protect the working girl.
EDGAR SMITH, *Heaven Will Protect the
Working Girl*

*"I should sooner give up my life,"* declared
Isabella, *"than surrender my virtue!"*

*"So be it!"* snarled the Count, drawing his
sword. *"Your life, then!"*

Secure in her hiding place between two
bookshelves at the rear of Minchin's Book
Emporium, Polly Hampton eagerly turned
the page of *The Wicked Count* and continued to read.

*"Oh, will no one save me?"* Isabella cried
piteously, clasping trembling hands to her
bosom. *"Would that I might —"*

"Why, Lady Helen, as I live and
breathe!"

Polly grimaced as a shrill greeting interrupted the thrilling confrontation between
the evil Count del Vecchio and the fair
Isabella.

"Good morning, Lady Farriday," returned a well-modulated voice. "How are you today?"

"Never better, my dear, never better. And if I may say so, you appear to be bearing up remarkably well."

"Is there any reason why I should not be?" Lady Helen sounded puzzled.

"Oh, none at all!" was Lady Farriday's hasty reply. "And how, pray, is your husband?"

"Mr. Brundy is quite well, thank you."

Marking her place with her finger, Polly peered around the shelves to glare unseen at the two ladies whose conversation made reading impossible. She recognized the elder and louder of the two, Lady Farriday, as a regular customer, but the younger, a regal beauty with hair the color of honey, was apparently a newcomer; at any rate, Polly could not recall having seen her before. Resolutely blocking out Lady Farriday's quite audible response, Polly returned to her book, only to be interrupted a second time by a voice even more difficult to ignore.

"*Guy Mannering*? Why yes, Sir Aubrey, indeed we have it, and all the other *Waverley* novels, as well." Although the bookshelf hid the speaker from view, Polly could imagine her employer fawning over his distinguished client. "You'll find it on the second shelf to your right. Miss Hampton will assist you."

As the sound of footsteps signaled the customer's approach, Polly shut her book with a snap and hastily returned it to the shelf. She quickly located the three leather-bound volumes and pulled them from the shelf just as a tall gentleman appeared between the rows. His artfully disarranged chestnut locks, double-breasted coat of Devonshire brown, tight-fitting biscuit breeches and cleverly tied cravat all bespoke the gentleman of fashion. Had she not been so aware of being caught shirking her duties, Polly might have stolen an admiring glance from under her lashes.

"Here you are, sir," she said breathlessly, offering him the books.

"Thank you."

Cool gray eyes flickered briefly in her direction as he accepted the proffered volumes and thumbed through their gold-edged pages for just a moment before taking his purchase to the counter. Alone once more between the shelves, Polly felt annoyed and not a little foolish. She might have known such a tulip of fashion would hardly be interested in the indiscretions of a mere shopgirl. Why, he had looked right through her as if she were invisible! Now she had lost her place in *The Wicked Count,* and all because of a worthless fribble with no thought in his head beyond the shine on his boots!

Not that she had any desire to receive his attentions, Polly reminded herself sternly. Those few girls of her station who had the misfortune to be so singled out generally found themselves in dire straits nine months later. Better that he should reserve his advances for those who wanted them, she thought, glowering from behind her bookshelf as he bowed over Lady Helen's hand.

"Poor Lady Helen," sighed Lady Farriday to her fellow patron, following the honey-blond beauty's departure with a pitying click of her tongue. "It pains me to see the duke's lovely daughter wed to that dreadful man, be he never so wealthy! Still, one must admire her stoicism, for she never utters a word of complaint."

"She seems happy enough," observed the gentleman. "So, for that matter, does her husband."

But Lady Farriday had no sympathy to waste on Lady Helen's spouse. "As well he might!" she said with a snort of derision. "A weaver, of all things, whose mother was no better than she should be — and God only knows who his father might be! They say he gave the duke one hundred thousand pounds for her, you know," she confided in a carrying whisper.

"My dear Lady Farriday, you behold me agog with curiosity," drawled the gentleman. "Who, pray, gave the duke one hundred thousand pounds — Mr. Brundy, his father, or the Almighty?"

"La, you were ever the wit, Sir Aubrey," tittered Lady Farriday, wagging a finger at him. "I know Mr. Brundy is a particular friend of yours, so I shall say no more on that head, but I must say it looks very odd for a man of your standing to keep such low company. A cousin of the Marquess of Inglewood on your mother's side, fraternizing with a common tradesman!"

"On the contrary, my lady, if he was indeed able to pay one hundred thousand pounds for a wife, I should rather call him an *un*common tradesman."

"But a tradesman nonetheless, and you are constantly in his company. How it must grieve your poor mama!"

"It does, indeed," Sir Aubrey acknowledged, inclining his stylishly cropped head. "But at least her efforts to reconfigure my circle of friends give her something with which to occupy her mind — something, that is, besides gossiping in bookstores."

Polly, who would have lost her position for such insolence, gasped quite audibly. But Lady Farriday had no interest in eavesdropping shopgirls, being fully occupied with glaring up at the impertinent Sir Aubrey before exiting the shop in a huff.

The door had no sooner closed behind her ladyship than Mr. Minchin, owner and proprietor of Minchin's Book Emporium, once more summoned Polly. Recalled to her duties, she retrieved her neglected feather duster and began to wield it with industry.

"Miss Hampton? Come here, Miss Hampton. I wish to speak to you."

"Yes, sir, Mr. Minchin," she called. "Right away, sir."

Polly hastily tucked a stray curl back into her ruffled cap and smoothed the front of her starched white apron, then followed her employer into his office. The cramped little room at the rear of the shop was furnished with a scarred desk, two straight chairs, and a seemingly endless assortment of papers and books. Sweeping a stack of these off one of the chairs, the shopkeeper motioned for her to be seated.

"Miss Hampton, as you are no doubt aware, the social season is ending, and many of our clients are leaving the Metropolis for Brighton or their country estates," Mr. Minchin began.

Polly, not quite sure what the social season had to do with her, merely nodded.

"Business has already fallen off considerably, and by August, Mayfair will be practically deserted," he continued. "Much as it pains me, I must reduce the size of my staff. Since you were the last one hired, it seems only fair that you should be the first released."

*Now I shall never know how Isabella escapes from the Count,* Polly thought irrelevantly as her benumbed brain struggled to grasp the enormity of her predicament. Since most shops only hired men, finding this position had seemed like a dream come true — and this was a rude awakening indeed. How would she ever find another position? As the gravity of her situation began to dawn, Polly clenched her hands tightly in her lap in an effort to subdue the panic which threatened to overtake her.

"Still, you have been an excellent worker for the four months you have been in my employ," Mr. Minchin assured her, as if conciliatory words would somehow sustain her through the lean days which loomed ahead. "Much of the nobility will return to

Town in the autumn when Parliament reconvenes. If you will check back with me at the end of September, perhaps I shall be able to offer you your old position back."

"That — that is very kind of you, Mr. Minchin," stammered Polly, her mind still reeling from the shock.

"There, there," he said, seating himself in the chair next to her so that he might drape a comforting arm about her shoulders. "I always take care of my girls, Polly. You're welcome to stay at my flat for as long as need be. I'm sure we can find something for you to do to earn your keep."

As his left hand kneaded her shoulder, his right hand patted hers in a manner which could only be described as familiar. His palm was moist and clammy, and his hot breath fanned her cheek. Suddenly she knew why Mr. Minchin was so eager to hire young women to work for him. She had been warned that evil abounded in the city, but in the tiny Leicestershire village of Littledean, such tales had been difficult to credit. Too late, it seemed, she discovered they were all too true.

"That won't be necessary, Mr. Minchin," she said, rising from her chair with great dignity. "If you will give me my wages, I had best be about the business of finding a new position."

Mr. Minchin's air of concern melted away, leaving in its place an ugly sneer. "I wish you luck in your search, Miss Hampton. Respectable positions are hard to come by, particularly for young females with no references." Seeing Polly's eyes widen, he explained. "I have long been aware of your penchant for reading during work hours, and while I am tolerant enough to make allowances for such behavior, other shopkeepers might not be so lenient. I could not in good conscience recommend you."

"My wages, Mr. Minchin," she reiterated, holding out her hand. Polly might lack references, but she was not without pride, and she refused to give him the satisfaction of seeing her grovel. However, upon seeing the pitifully small number of coins he counted into her outstretched palm, she was moved to protest. "This is not the amount we agreed upon four months ago!"

"You haven't worked the full week," he reminded her. "And what about the apron and cap you're wearing? Did you think those things were free? No, Miss Hampton, I have a goodly sum invested in my employees. When one proves unsatisfactory, I must recoup my losses."

Without another word, Polly stripped off the apron and ripped the cap from her head. "In that case, you may keep them," she replied with false bravado, dumping the discarded garments onto her erstwhile employer's lap. "I'm sure you will look lovely in them."

Clutching the coins tightly in her fist, Polly collected her shawl and bonnet and exited the tiny office, but not quickly enough to avoid hearing Mr. Minchin's parting shot.

"I shall call on you in the workhouse a few weeks hence, Miss Hampton. I have a feeling by that time you may have changed your mind."

*He is only trying to frighten me,* she told herself, blinking back tears. *But I will not cry. I am a great lady, at least on my father's side, and a lady would never so demean herself.*

Nevertheless, her eyes filled in spite of her best efforts to keep her emotions in check. Head bowed to conceal her distress, she had almost reached the front door of the shop when she collided with a well-tailored coat of Devonshire brown.

"Here now, watch your step," admonished its wearer, as slender but strong fingers closed over Polly's arms.

Glancing up, she saw Sir Aubrey, startled out of his habitually bored expression.

"I say, miss, are you all right?"

"Quite all right — I beg your pardon — so clumsy of me —"

Wresting herself free of his grasp, she stumbled out of the shop and into the street, neither knowing nor caring where her feet took her, until at last, winded and panting, she was forced to stop for breath. As her breathing gradually became less labored, she became aware of her surroundings, and found herself standing before a milliner's shop, staring unseeing at her reflection in the glass. As her gaze focused, she became aware of light blue eyes dilated with fear looking back at her from a face framed by riotous red-gold curls.

Other young women might have been pleased with the image reflected in the glass, but Polly saw there only a reminder of how dismally she had failed. She had come to London to search for a similar face, and had found nothing but disappointment and now poverty. Her mama, God rest her soul, had warned her to stay away from London, as had the kindly vicar who had taken her in after her mother's death, but Polly had been adamant. By her mother's own admission, there existed somewhere among fashionable London society a gentleman whose likeness she bore. She had been convinced that she had only to confront the mystery man to make him, if not acknowledge her publicly as his own, at least provide some modest stipend for her so that she might repay Reverend Jennings for his kindness. When Mr. Minchin gave her a position at his shop, she was convinced it was only a matter of time before her father walked through the door. The only question remaining was who would be the first to recognize whom.

It had made perfect sense when she had first hatched the scheme after reading the popular gothic romance *The Lost Heir*. In the book, the hero Leandro and his father had enjoyed a tearful reunion, Leandro had married his true love Dolores, and everyone had lived happily ever after. But after four months, Polly had been forced to admit that, if her father were indeed in London, he had never read *The Lost Heir*; certainly no likely gentleman had entered the portals of Minchin's Book Emporium.

With the loss of her position, however, the task of finding her father must yield to the more pressing demands of keeping food in her belly and a roof over her head. Squaring her shoulders and thrusting her chin forward, she opened the door of the milliner's shop and marched inside to inquire after a position.

She repeated the process frequently on her way home, but the answers to her queries were variations on the same theme: with the migration of the *beau monde* from Town, no new workers were being hired. By the time she reached Henrietta Street, where she lived with a linen-draper's family in a hired room over his shop, her spirits were utterly downcast. She had lost her old position and had no hope of finding a new one. She had no choice but to swallow her pride and return home in defeat — if, in fact, her meager store of coins would stretch to the cost of a ticket on the stagecoach.

The bell over the door of Hargett & Son, Linen-drapers, jingled as she entered the shop, its cheerful music a sharp contrast to Polly's dispirited sigh. If only she had thought before flinging her apron and cap back at Mr. Minchin! They might have fetched a few pence at a used-clothing shop. But the provocation had been too great to resist, and she had always been impulsive to a fault; indeed, good Reverend Jennings had often said it was her besetting sin. Now, besides admitting that her impulsive trip to London had been but one more of her rash starts, she would have to endure the added humiliation of requesting the vicar to send her money he could ill afford for the return trip.

And he would do it, too, she thought with a sudden rush of affection for the man who had stood *in loco parentis* to her for the last six years. He would send her the needed funds over his wife's objections, and never utter a word of censure.

"Why, Miss Hampton, you're home early," observed her landlord, Mr. Hargett. "My Tom will be sorry he missed you," he added with a broad wink.

"Business was slower than usual," she answered vaguely, unwilling to reveal the whole truth just yet. Mr. and Mrs. Hargett were kindly enough people, but Tom Hargett, the junior half of Hargett & Son, had been making sheep's eyes at her almost from the day of her arrival, and his fond parents lost no opportunity to let her know how much they would welcome a match between their only son and their genteel young boarder. Polly doubted they would be so cruel as to turn her out immediately, but remaining under their roof now that she could no longer pay her keep would make it exceedingly awkward to repulse their son's ever more pressing advances. And so she said nothing of her misfortunes, but watched as Mr. Hargett artfully draped a bolt of fabric the better to catch a customer's eye.

"Pretty," she remarked, fingering the crisp folds of printed cotton.

"That's the future you're looking at," the loquacious Mr. Hargett informed her. "So far as I know, it's the first fabric to be woven and printed all under the same roof. A man named Brundy produces it at a mill near Manchester, and I'll wager it won't be long before every textile mill in the North will be doing the same. I met the fellow myself many years ago, when the old man — Mr. Brundy that was — brought him to London to show him this end of the business. He couldn't have been more than eighteen years old at the time, but already he was as shrewd as he could stare. Of course, his name wasn't Brundy then — he changed it when the old man died and left him the mill, lock, stock, and barrel."

"His family must have been pleased at his good fortune." Polly feigned an interest she did not feel, grateful that Mr. Hargett had apparently dropped the subject of young Tom.

"Oh, he had no family. That's what made his story so unusual. The old Mr. Brundy got him from the workhouse when he was only a tadpole."

The mention of the workhouse brought unpleasant memories to bear. Polly, unwilling to face those memories just yet, sought to stifle them by seizing upon the familiar name.

"I heard some mention of a Mr. Brundy in the bookshop today," she remarked when her landlord paused to draw a breath.

Mr. Hargett grinned knowingly. "Oh, there's been gossip a-plenty about Mr. Brundy since he married a duke's daughter and set himself up as a gentleman in Grosvenor Square. Bookstores aren't the only place where fashionable customers talk, you know," he added with a mischievous twinkle in his eye.

"No, I suppose not," she said with an answering smile before heading for the back stairs. Suddenly she longed for the privacy of her room and the opportunity to rest for a moment before facing the task of composing a suitably penitent letter to Reverend Jennings.

"Crump!"

Mr. Hargett's exclamation interrupted her flight, and she turned back.

"I beg your pardon?"

"Crump, his name was. Ethan Crump," he said, pleased beyond bearing at this feat of memory. "Isn't it funny, the things the mind recalls after so many years?"

"Funny, indeed," Polly agreed, and climbed the narrow staircase to her room, a cramped chamber furnished with a bed, a rickety washstand bearing a pitcher and basin, a single straight chair, and a writing table over which a cracked mirror was hung. She removed her bonnet and hung her shawl on a peg behind the door, then collapsed onto her bed. She had not the luxury of a long repose if she hoped to make the day's post. She rose quickly, washed her face with water from the basin, and sat down to write. She struggled with this epistle, as she could not spare more than a single sheet of paper in the attempt and thus had to choose every word with care, but at last it was finished. She folded it and sealed it with a wafer, and was about to take it downstairs to be mailed when a knock fell upon her door.

"Miss Hampton?" The voice belonged to Mrs. Hargett, her landlady. "You have a letter, dear."

So she had missed the post, after all. Somehow this relatively minor setback seemed perfectly in keeping with everything else that had happened to her. She opened the door and took the letter, then broke the seal and spread the single sheet.

She glanced down at the signature first, and found that the sender was Mrs. Jennings, the vicar's wife. The discovery was enough to fill Polly with foreboding, since Mrs. Jennings had never approved of her husband's generosity to one born in sin and had never hesitated to voice her views on the subject, so long as her husband was not there to chide her for her lack of Christian charity.

As Polly deciphered the spidery script, she felt decidedly unwell. It pained Mrs. Jennings to inform her that Mr. Jennings had been carried off quite suddenly by an infectious fever of the lungs . . . They could be thankful that his sufferings, though severe, were not of a long duration . . . It would mean so much to him to know that Polly was well established in London . . . As for herself, she would now be making her home with her widowed sister in Hampshire . . .

There was no mention of the location of this sister's house, nor anything else that might be construed as an invitation for Polly to join her there. The message was clear: Polly was now "well established in London," and Mrs. Jennings considered any obligation on her part to have been fully discharged. There was no home to go back to, even had she possessed the funds to do so.

## 2

A man's house is his castle.
SIR EDWARD COKE, *Third Institute*

"Miss Hampton? Are you all right, dear?" asked Mrs. Hargett, watching in unabashed curiosity as her boarder turned pale upon reading the missive. "Not bad news, I hope?"

"No, Mrs. Hargett, merely surprising," Polly stammered, hastily refolding the letter and tucking it into her bodice, safe from her landlady's prying eyes. "It appears I will be leaving you soon."

"Leaving?" echoed Mrs. Hargett. "Whatever for?"

*Because I can no longer afford to pay for my room,* Polly might have said. But her grief was too raw, and her future too uncertain, to allow her to confide in anyone as yet. Instead, she fixed her features in a smile and said, with a fair semblance of eagerness, "Only fancy, Mrs. Hargett! I've been offered a new position in a fine house!"

Mrs. Hargett's somewhat protuberant eyes narrowed in suspicion. "And was it a fine gentleman offered you this new position?"

Polly, accurately interpreting Mrs. Hargett's inferences, blushed rosily. "The position is that of — of companion to an elderly lady. I had the privilege of serving her in the bookstore one day, and she liked the way I read aloud," she added, her landlady's skepticism spurring her on to new heights of creativity.

Mrs. Hargett clicked her tongue reproachfully. " 'Companion,' my eye! The best position for a pretty young thing like you is to be wife to a handsome young man who'll provide for you decent. My Tom will inherit his father's business one day, you know," she said pointedly.

"I hope for Mr. Hargett's sake that that day is far into the future," Polly replied, ignoring her landlady's insinuations.

"Oh, to be sure! But don't you be thinking that Tom'll not have a penny to call his own until then! Lawks, no! He's more nor capable of supporting a wife — aye, and a couple o' young 'uns, too, come to that!"

As Mr. Hargett's establishment did a thriving business, Polly could not dispute this statement; unfortunately, Tom's wife would have to accept along with his successful business and respectable income a husband whose character was reflected all too clearly in his bovine countenance. But of course Tom's doting mama could not be expected to welcome the information that Polly had known cows with more intelligence than her son, and so Polly doggedly packed her meager possessions into a battered valise, paid her disapproving landlady for her last week's rent, and set out to face an uncertain future.

Having already exhausted the possibility of finding work in a shop, she was obliged to lower her sights to domestic work in a private house. For one who had been reminded all her life that she was Quality, at least on her father's side, this was a comedown indeed, but after examining her options, Polly came to the conclusion that respectable work polishing silver, making beds, or even sweeping out grates was preferable to the sort of position which Mr. Minchin proposed. Her flagging spirits were somewhat bolstered by the slim but ever-present hope that her father might visit the house in which she found employment, and so she set off on foot for the more fashionable residential districts, her valise banging against her knee with every step.

Alas, here too it seemed fate was against her. At her first stop, the housekeeper inspected her hands and, finding them soft and white, pronounced that she had never known a day's work in her life — a false accusation which, due to her lack of references, Polly was unable to disprove. Her second attempt appeared more promising, at least at first, for here the housekeeper invited her in and instructed her to take off her bonnet and shawl. When Polly obeyed, she was ordered to turn around. She sketched a slow circle under the woman's watchful gaze, at the end of which the housekeeper said, "His lordship sent you, did he?"

"His lordship, ma'am?" echoed Polly, all at sea.

"Aye, he always did have an eye for a pretty young thing, although I'll admit you're a bit more ladylike than most."

"I'm afraid I don't quite —"

"Well, you tell my lord that he'll have to set you up in a house of your own, for her ladyship will eat me for breakfast if I help him install one of his fancy-pieces under his own roof, and no mistake!"

Finding her bonnet and shawl thrust into her arms, Polly wasted no time defending herself against false charges, but beat a hasty retreat, helped on her way by the offended housekeeper. Her next stop had certain similarities to this one, the main difference being that it was not the master but the eldest son who was known to raid the kitchen at night for things other than bread and cheese. Subsequent attempts were equally fruitless. Many of the houses had already been closed for the summer, the door knockers removed and the servants dispatched to their masters' country estates or released to find other employment in Town.

Alone on the sidewalk, Polly dropped her valise to the pavement and collapsed wearily onto it. The sun was beginning to sink in the west, and she had nowhere to go, save back to the Hargetts and their dim-witted Tom. If only she had been successful in her search for her father, how different her life might have been! As it was, she could almost see the doors of the workhouse yawning wide to receive her. Would she be so determined to defend her honor after a few weeks in that living hell, or would she leap at Mr. Minchin's offer? For it was common knowledge that once one entered those dreaded portals, escape was well nigh impossible.

Except, of course, that one *had* escaped.

Mr. Hargett had described him at great length, and Lady Farriday had spoken of him to the fashionable gentleman in the bookstore. Perhaps, having a similar history, he might be willing to help her find her father. But no, according to Lady Farriday, Mr. Brundy was an unscrupulous businessman who had used his wealth to coerce the beautiful Lady Helen into marriage — hardly the sort of man upon whose mercy one might throw oneself. Still, begging charity from a stranger was preferable to the few other options which presented themselves, and so Polly rose wearily to her feet and tightened her grip on her valise.

Deciding that it would not be at all the thing to trudge to fashionable Grosvenor Square on foot, she was obliged to part with one of her precious coins in order to hire a hackney to take her to her destination. Alas, not until she was set down in that modish neighborhood did she realize that she had no idea which one of the imposing residences lining the square housed the man about whom she had heard so much.

"Excuse me," she called to the crossing sweeper plying his trade on the corner, "do you know which one of these houses belongs to a Mr. Ethan Brundy?"

"Aye, miss, that I do," he replied, and turned back to his broom.

With a little huff of annoyance, Polly sacrificed another coin to the cause.

"That would be number twenty-three," he said, jerking a thumb in the right direction with one hand while he pocketed her hard-earned pay with the other.

Polly thanked him curtly and set off down the street in the direction he had indicated. When she reached her destination, however, the stately pilastered façade gave her pause. This was not the sort of building one might expect to house a weaver. Mr. Brundy must be very, very wealthy indeed. Why, the Prince Regent himself would feel at home in such a house!

Squaring her shoulders, she marched gamely up the steps, lifted the brass knocker, and let it fall. A moment later the door opened to reveal a daunting figure in black coat and knee breeches. He was older than she had imagined, but in all other aspects, his appearance was every bit as forbidding as she had been led to believe.

"Mr. Brundy?" she asked uncertainly.

"My name is Evers," the man informed

her with great dignity. "I am the butler."

"Oh," said Polly, quite cowed. In retrospect, she should have known that the wealthy Mr. Brundy would not answer his own door, but then she knew little of *ton* ways beyond what she had seen in Mr. Minchin's shop and read between the pages of the books on his shelves. "I — I should like to see Mr. Brundy, if you please."

Evers's seasoned eye assessed the visitor at a glance. She did not look like a lady of Quality, if her dark stuff gown and frumpy bonnet were anything to judge by, and yet four months in Mr. Brundy's employ had taught him not to set too much store by appearances. Opening the door wider, he bade the visitor enter.

Had she paused in her negotiations with the crossing sweeper long enough to cast a glance back up the Square, Polly might have witnessed Mr. Ethan Brundy, mill owner and canny investor on 'Change, entering his Grosvenor Street domicile. Once inside, he surrendered his hat and gloves to the butler and inquired after his wife. Upon being informed that he might find her ladyship in the dining room, he betook himself up the stairs in this direction.

It had been five years since he had inherited the mill that had made him, at the tender age of three-and-twenty, one of England's wealthiest men, but when he took the time to reflect upon the turns his life had taken, he still marveled. He had been only nine years old when Mr. Brundy, requiring cheap labor for his mill, had plucked him from the workhouse, and so his memories of that bleak existence were perhaps mercifully vague. Nevertheless, he had clear recollections of being always hungry, always cold, and, although surrounded by persons of all ages as miserable as himself, always alone. Now he had as much as he wanted to eat, whenever he wanted to eat it (small wonder that his tailor bemoaned the fact that Mr. Brundy's waist was not so narrow as fashion dictated!), he kept fires burning in every room which he might conceivably wish to enter, and he slept — more often than not — with the former Lady Helen Radney in his arms. The thought made him impatient for nightfall, and he quickened his pace as he climbed the stairs.

Although it was too early for dinner, he did indeed find his wife in the dining room, arranging flowers in a bowl for the center of the table. As her back was to the door, she was unaware of his presence, and he, seizing upon the advantage of surprise, slipped up behind her and wrapped his arms about her waist.

"I'm 'ome, 'elen," he said, nuzzling her neck.

Lady Helen, displaying the stoicism for which she had been praised that very morning, submitted to this assault on her person with a compliance which even the sympathetic Lady Farriday would have deemed excessive.

"Ethan, the servants will see us," she protested half-heartedly, leaning back against her husband and cradling the arms that imprisoned her.

"Let 'em see," was his reply. "If they 'aven't figured out by now that I'm 'ead over ears in love with me wife, they're too stupid to be working for me, anyway."

They were already two months wed, but had lived as man and wife for only half that long, and he still found her maidenly modesty enchanting, secure in the knowledge that he could coax her out of it later, in the privacy of the bedchamber.

At length, however, her heightened senses detected something not quite right about the sleeve of his coat beneath her fingers. Freeing herself abruptly, she turned to cast a disapproving eye over his baggy coat, whereupon he pulled her against him in a face-to-face embrace.

"Ethan!" she scolded, putting up only a token resistance to this high-handed treatment. "While I have no objection to you dressing for comfort in the privacy of your own home, you promised to wear coats that fit properly when you are out and about in public!"

"I'd 'ardly consider a visit to me ware'ouse a social call," he protested.

"For that matter, I would hardly call it a *visit*," retorted Lady Helen. "You've been gone all day."

"Aye, that I 'ave," agreed her much-maligned spouse. "I'd a few things to take care of before we leave for Brighton in the morning. I want no interruptions on me 'oneymoon," he added, covering her mouth with his own before she could voice further grievances.

Lady Helen, however, could find nothing in these sentiments with which to take issue, and so returned his kiss with every appearance of enthusiasm.

And so it was that Evers, after admitting the visitor to the hall and taking her bonnet and shawl, climbed the stairs to the dining room and discovered master and mistress locked in a passionate embrace. This had become a common occurrence over the last month, and in that time Evers had perfected the art of becoming blind and deaf. Stepping back into the corridor, he cleared his throat quite audibly to notify them of his presence before reentering the room. The tableau which met his eyes this time was quite different. Lady Helen's floral arrangement evidently possessed her undivided attention, although her heightened color and the gleam in her husband's eye betrayed their interrupted embrace.

"Begging your pardon, sir," Evers addressed Mr. Brundy, "but there is a young, er, person below who is wishful of seeing you."

"A 'person,' Evers? Don't be so vague! 'oo is 'e?"

Evers felt obliged to correct his employer's erroneous assumption. "*She,* sir. Owing to the unexpected nature of the young woman's arrival, I fear I neglected to inquire as to her name. Shall I do so now?"

"No, just show 'er into the drawing room. I'll be there directly."

Bowing his acquiescence, Evers betook himself from the room, only to climb the stairs again a moment later with Polly in tow. That intrepid young lady trudged upward in the butler's wake, trying valiantly not to gawk at the opulence of her surroundings, from the elaborate plasterwork ceilings over her head to the thick Aubusson carpet beneath her feet. Only now, when it was too late to turn back, did the enormity of her undertaking begin to dawn. Surely it was unlikely that any man living in such a house could feel any degree of sympathy for an unknown and penniless girl! Dear, good Reverend Jennings, on the other hand, might not have lived in grandeur, but he would have given his last crust of bread to any soul in need. Polly grieved anew for the one person who might have acted in the place of a male relation and shielded her from men like Mr. Minchin.

At the top of the stairs Evers opened the door of the drawing room, and Polly entered a tastefully appointed chamber whose understated elegance made her feel hopelessly dowdy. An oil portrait whose subject she recognized as Lady Helen hung over the mantel and the painted image, dressed all in white and wearing a dazzling necklace of diamonds, seemed to sneer disapprovingly at the uninvited guest. Spying a gilt-framed mirror on the opposite wall, she took stock of her appearance, and found her worst suspicions confirmed. She smoothed her rumpled dark skirts, which had been hopelessly crushed from her hackney ride, and was in the process of slicking back her disheveled curls when the door opened to reveal the honey-haired beauty from the bookstore.

However, it was not Lady Helen but the man beside her who commanded Polly's full attention. Although not above the average height, he was more solidly built than most of the fashionable gentlemen who patronized Mr. Minchin's shop, and his mulberry colored coat, while obviously cut from the finest cloth, was so baggy it might have been made for a much stouter man. His dark curly hair, though fashionably cropped, was somewhat disheveled. He was not handsome at all, at least not in the sense that the gentleman in the bookstore had been handsome. It would have been hard to imagine a less likely husband for the elegantly beautiful Lady Helen. If this were indeed Mr. Brundy, she could see why Lady Farriday had been so appalled. And yet there was something inviting about his welcoming smile and warm brown eyes, something that belied Lady Farriday's gothic whisperings of coercion and brutality. To Polly, he looked more brotherly than brutal. Brotherly . . . And she was in desperate need of a male relation. . . .

"Mr. Brundy?" Her voice shook on the words.

"Aye, that I am," he answered.

"Ethan!" she exclaimed, smiling uncertainly at him. "Don't you know me? But of course you could not! I'm your sister!"

## 3

Marriage is a desperate thing.
JOHN SELDEN, *Table Talk*

*"Sister?"* echoed Mr. Brundy. Gone was any trace of the welcoming warmth she thought she had seen in his eyes, and the frigid contempt which replaced it was sufficient to convince Polly that, if anything, Lady Farriday had been too generous in her assessment of his character.

"Ethan!" cried Lady Helen, clasping Polly's hands warmly. "You never told me you had a sister!"

"Life is just full of surprises," he muttered in skeptical tones.

"Do come and sit down," she urged, steering Polly toward a striped satin sofa. "Only fancy, Ethan, if your sister had come a day later, she would have found us gone."

"What a shame *that* would've been," was his less than enthusiastic reply.

Lady Helen, fully occupied in seeing her new-found relation comfortably disposed on the sofa, made no reply to her husband, but instead inquired as to her guest's name.

"Polly," replied the visitor, watching from under demurely lowered eyelashes to observe the effect of this pronouncement on Mr. Brundy. "Polly Crump."

His reaction was swift and profound. Indeed, as Evers later confided to an enthralled Cook, the master might have been turned to stone before his very eyes.

"Polly *Crump,* did you say?"

"Ethan, what is the matter?" asked Lady Helen, observing her husband's distress.

He stared with unseeing eyes at his wife's anxious face. "Crump was me mum's name — and mine, before I took the name of Brundy."

"Then it is hardly surprising for your sister to share it," Lady Helen pointed out reasonably. Then, spying a curious Evers still hovering in the doorway, she sent him about his business. "Evers, have Miss Crump's things brought up to the blue bedchamber, and tell Cook that we will be increasing our covers for dinner."

As Evers quit the room, Mr. Brundy seized his wife's hand and quickly followed suit.

"A word with you, 'elen, me dear," he growled, half-dragging her into the corridor and firmly shutting the door behind her. "What, pray, do you think you're doing?"

"Why, trying to make your sister feel at home," she said, baffled by his odd behavior.

"I 'aven't got a sister," he informed her.

"I don't understand you, Ethan. I should have thought you would *want* a family of your own."

"I've all the family I need in you, 'elen," he said, more gently this time.

"But your sister —"

" 'elen, five years ago, I in'erited a cotton mill. Overnight I was a wealthy man, and suddenly I'd more relatives than I could count — each with an 'ard-luck story and an 'and 'eld out."

Lady Helen's green eyes grew round. "You think Miss Crump is lying?"

"I don't just think it, love. I know she is."

"But she knew your birth name — something your own wife didn't know, for that matter," she reminded him.

"Oh, she's thorough, I'll grant 'er that. I'd give a monkey to know where she got 'er information."

"But Ethan, we can hardly toss her out into the street!"

"Watch me," said Mr. Brundy, reaching for the doorknob.

"Wait!" Moving quickly to block his

path, Lady Helen grasped the lapels of his baggy coat. "Darling, I haven't forgotten how perfectly dreadful I was to you when you first came to Town. I don't want to make the same mistake with your sister."

"That girl is no more me sister than *you* are!" he insisted. "Tell me, 'ow old would you say me 'sister' is?"

Lady Helen considered the question. "Very nearly my own age, I should say. Perhaps a little younger — nineteen or twenty."

"Which would mean she must be at least eight years younger than I am," he concluded. "But me mum died when I was six. Unless she found a way to bear a child two years after 'er death —"

"But what if your mother didn't die, Ethan?" asked Lady Helen as a new thought struck her. "What if she discovered she was to have another child, and hoped to prevail upon the father to marry her, so —"

Mr. Brundy stared at his wife as if she had just struck him. "You're saying me mum put me in the work'ouse because I was in the way!"

Seeing his stricken look, she quickly backed away from a suggestion that could only bring her husband pain. Although she

44

still did not consider such a scenario beyond the realm of possibility, she would not hurt him for the world. "Or perhaps she was not dead," she added hastily. "Perhaps she was very ill, or — or injured, and only recovered after you had already been taken from her —"

"Or per'aps I'm being taken advantage of by a scheming little adventuress 'oo wants to get 'er 'ands on me money," he finished for her.

"But what could she possibly hope to gain by such a deception?"

"Think of it, love: I'm a rich man, probably the only such in England with no way of disproving her claims, and me wife is the daughter of a dook. Depend on it, she thinks she's found a way to foist 'erself onto Society."

"Like *you* did, in other words," was Lady Helen's observation.

"At least I paid me own way!" pointed out her husband.

"And could do the same for a dozen others, if you wished!"

"Aye, but I *don't* wish!" retorted Mr. Brundy.

"No, you would deny your sister the same privileges that you take for granted! I never knew you could be so — so *selfish!*"

"I am not selfish, and that girl is not me sister! For God's sake, *look* at 'er! We don't look anything alike!"

Until that moment, Lady Helen had never heard her husband raise his voice, and was momentarily taken aback by his vehemence. "Shhh! She'll hear you!" she urged, glancing furtively at the closed door. "In any case, Ethan, many people bear little resemblance to their siblings. Perhaps she resembles your mother instead."

"*I* resemble me mother! That's why she could never be certain 'oo me father was."

"Well, of one thing I am certain: it is not at all the thing for us to leave your sister cooling her heels in the drawing room while we argue in the corridor," replied Lady Helen, and turned to open the door.

"For the last time, 'elen, that girl is not me sister!" Mr. Brundy ground out through clenched teeth. "And I'll be 'anged if I'll do the pretty over dinner with the scheming little hussy!"

"In that case, we shall miss you, Mr. Brundy," Lady Helen said placidly, and swept into the drawing room, every inch the duke's daughter.

As darkness fell over Mayfair, the stately

46

homes of Belgrave Square fairly blazed with light while inside, their fashionable residents prepared themselves for pleasures abroad. A shaft of light spilled into the street as the front door of one of these abodes was opened, momentarily silhouetting the fashionably dressed gentleman within before the door closed behind him, leaving him alone in the gaslit street.

In a gesture oddly out of keeping with his elegant evening attire, Sir Aubrey Tabor sagged momentarily against the iron railings fronting the house, breathing an audible sigh of relief. He had survived the obligatory weekly dinner with his widowed mother, during which he had been treated to a lengthy diatribe on his responsibility to increase and multiply. Furthermore, the dowager Lady Tabor had recommended one Lady Jane Cunningham for his partner in this endeavor. Nothing, not even the gift of a book which Sir Aubrey had purchased that very day in an admittedly craven attempt to forestall just such a lecture, had diverted the good lady's mind.

Now, dismissed at last from the matriarchal presence, he found himself in dire need of sympathetic (meaning male) companionship. With this end in view, he shouldered his ebony walking stick and set his feet in the direction of Brooks's in St. James Street. After surrendering his hat and gloves to the porter, he climbed the stairs to the card room and joined the crowd gathered around the macao table. Although the company was convivial enough, Sir Aubrey's luck was out, and he soon found himself punting on tick.

"Deuced ill luck, Sir Aubrey," commiserated the knightly sexagenarian Sir Linus Hewitt after one such losing hand. "But perhaps you are lucky in love, instead."

"Indeed, I am *very* lucky in that I am unburdened by that most inconvenient of emotions," agreed Sir Aubrey, wondering if the urge to marry off their juniors was characteristic of his mother's generation.

Sir Linus laughed heartily. "So cynical, at such a tender age! That will change soon enough, I trow!"

"I am thirty!" retorted Sir Aubrey.

"A mere boy," chortled Sir Linus, glancing toward the door as yet another gentleman entered the card room. "Ah, now here's a fellow whose example you might look to!"

Sir Aubrey opened his mouth to deliver a crushing snub, but upon recognizing the newcomer, he decided Sir Linus was not worth the effort. "I say, Ethan, come have a drop!" he called to the late arrival, snapping his fingers for a waiter. "*Garçon!* Another bottle of brandy, and an extra glass!"

So summoned, Mr. Brundy ambled over to the macao table to observe his friend's progress. The Honourable Robert Jemison obligingly moved aside to make room for him, remarking jovially as he did so, "Well, well, Brundy, we don't usually have the pleasure of seeing you here of an evening. Have you tired of living under the cat's foot?"

"I've 'ad business at 'ome to attend to," Mr. Brundy replied more curtly than was his wont.

"Aye, I remember when I was first wed," said Sir Linus with a reminiscent gleam in his eye. "As I recall, I often had business at home to attend to, as well — and nine months later, a son bawling lustily in the nursery!"

A great deal of bawdy laughter greeted this sally, but Mr. Brundy neither refuted nor confirmed the implication. In fact, when he spoke, it was not to Sir Linus at all, but to Lord Carteret, who held the bank.

"Deal me in," he said tersely, tossing off his brandy in a single gulp.

Sir Aubrey had been listening to the old

knight's jests as appreciatively as anyone, but upon hearing this utterance, his mouth dropped open so far that his chin nearly grazed the floor. It was well known that Mr. Brundy never gambled; in fact, Sir Aubrcy was one of the few who knew about the high-stakes game in which Mr. Brundy had wagered his cotton mill against his wife's diamond necklace, which had fallen into the hands of the unscrupulous earl of Waverly.

"Are you feeling all right, Ethan?" asked Sir Aubrey in some concern.

"Never better," answered Mr. Brundy in a voice which dared anyone to suggest otherwise.

A fine instinct for self-preservation warned Sir Aubrey not to press the issue, and play was resumed without further comment. Mr. Brundy won the first hand, but seemed even more displeased with his winnings than Sir Aubrey had with his losses. He scowled impatiently at the pile of coins Lord Carteret pushed across the table to him and, with a recklessness which both fascinated and horrified Sir Aubrey, he staked all his winnings on the next hand. When it, too, proved a winner, he pushed back his chair in disgust.

"No more for me, gentlemen," he said,

then collected the pile of coins and rose from the table.

"Quitting so soon?" asked Mr. Jemison.

"No need to be selfish, Brundy," chided Sir Linus jovially. "You might at least share the wealth — you certainly have enough of it to go around."

Mr. Brundy made as if to reply, then thought better of it, settling instead for clenching his jaw and leaving the other players without so much as a fare-thee-well.

Sir Aubrey, by this time convinced beyond all doubt that something was troubling his friend, followed and ran his quarry to earth in the reading room, where he was glaring at the financial page of the *Times* with so fierce an expression that Sir Aubrey would not have been surprised had it burst into flames.

"Have you heard the news, Ethan?" he asked with studied nonchalance. "The latest *on dit* has it that your nemesis, Lord Waverly, has skipped to the Continent to elude his creditors."

Mr. Brundy's only reply was a noncommittal grunt.

"Not to pry, old fellow," Sir Aubrey persisted, "but what's eating you?"

Mr. Brundy's gaze shifted from his

newspaper to his friend while he debated what answer, if any, to return. Good friend though he was, Sir Aubrey would not have been his confidante of choice; that would be Lord David Markham, a rising member of Parliament whose successful campaign he had funded. Unfortunately, Lord David had recently married, and had promptly borne his bride off to Paris. Lord David, he reflected morosely, had the right idea.

By contrast, Sir Aubrey was a confirmed bachelor with inclinations toward dandyism, who was far more concerned with the fall of his cravat than the vacant nursery at Tabor Hall — hardly a promising source to turn to for help with difficulties of a marital nature. Still, Sir Aubrey was possessed of a pair of functioning ears, and had professed a willingness to use them. Mr. Brundy elected to avail himself of the opportunity to vent his spleen.

"Tell me, Aubrey, would you say I'm a selfish man?"

"Is that what's troubling you?" Sir Aubrey dismissed his friend's concerns with a wave of his slender, aristocratic hand. "Pay no heed to Sir Linus; he's more than a trifle bosky, you know."

" 'Twasn't Sir Linus I'm thinking on.

'elen 'urled the same accusation at me earlier this evening."

"Oho!" exclaimed Sir Aubrey with a knowing grin. "So the honeymoon is over, is it?"

"In this case, it 'adn't even begun," confessed Mr. Brundy. "We leave for Brighton in the morning — all three of us," he added darkly.

If it were possible, Sir Aubrey's grin grew wider. "Three?"

"Aye, laugh if you must! A girl turned up on me doorstep this evening, claiming to be me sister. I know she's lying, but 'elen will 'ave it the girl is on the up and up."

"How can you be so sure she isn't?" asked Sir Aubrey. "Nothing against your mother, Ethan, but if she had one child out of wedlock, why couldn't she have had another?"

"Because me mum was cold in 'er grave long before this chit ever walked God's earth!" retorted Mr. Brundy, annoyed at being presented with the same argument his wife had put forward. "Added to that, we don't look anything alike. The girl's got blue eyes, and 'er 'air's a sort of reddish yellow."

Sir Aubrey's amusement turned to genuine interest. "Indeed? It sounds as if you have a beauty on your hands."

"A beauty?" Mr. Brundy considered the matter as if such a possibility had never occurred to him. "I suppose she's pretty enough. What further proof would you need that she's no kin of mine?" he concluded with a rueful smile.

"That settles it! If you, who can see no woman beyond your own wife, find this girl pretty enough, she must be a diamond of the first water! I suddenly find myself possessed of a burning desire to see this supposed sister of yours."

"I'd give 'er to you with me blessing, but 'elen won't 'ear of it. She's convinced the girl is me sister, and must stay with us."

"Ethan, for a married man, you know amazingly little about women!" declared Sir Aubrey, shaking his head in pitying disbelief.

"And you, I suppose, are an expert on the subject," Mr. Brundy remarked cynically.

"Can you doubt it? I have, after all, successfully evaded the creatures for thirty years."

"Your day will come, Aubrey, mark me words," Mr. Brundy predicted confidently.

"You are beginning to sound like Sir Linus," Sir Aubrey informed him. "Nevertheless, I should like to know why, if marriage is the blissful state you would have me believe, you are sulking about here while Lady Helen is no doubt crying into her pillow."

This was a possibility Mr. Brundy had not considered. "Do you really think so?" he asked, torn between distress at having caused his wife pain and hope that, if she were half as miserable as he was, a reconciliation might yet be effected.

"Trust me, Ethan, they always cry," drawled Sir Aubrey.

"I've no wish to 'urt me wife," said Mr. Brundy.

"Of course you do not! The trick is to bring the thing off in such a way that you come out looking like a hero to Lady Helen."

"And 'ow, pray, am I to do that?"

"Ethan, do you remember when you first came to London?"

Mr. Brundy remembered his inauspicious introduction to Society very well, since it had taken place only a few months previously. He had quickly discovered that England's elite class was extremely reluctant to clasp a weaver to its bosom — and none more reluctant than Lady Helen Radney, the woman with whom he had fallen in love at first sight. Fortunately, by the time he realized how impossible such a match would be, he had already married her.

"Aye, I remember it well," he said at last, a little smile playing about his mouth.

"The less pleasant parts, I mean," said Sir Aubrey, correctly interpreting his friend's beatific expression. "To be blunt, Ethan, no one knows better than you how brutal Society can be to outsiders. Your membership at Brooks's taxed all David's powers of diplomacy, and in spite of Lady Helen's ducal connections, there are still families who won't receive you."

"Thank you for pointing that out to me," said Mr. Brundy, his voice heavy with irony. "Now that you've put me in me place, would you mind telling me what that's got to do with this girl?"

Sir Aubrey's smile turned demonic. "If she wants to cut a dash in Society under your aegis, let her. She'll turn tail and run the first time I scowl at her through my quizzing glass."

"You'd do that for me?" asked Mr. Brundy, much struck.

"I'm a closet romantic," drawled Sir Aubrey.

By the time Mr. Brundy returned to

Grosvenor Square, the hour was far advanced, but his spirits were somewhat lighter. He expected Lady Helen to have long since sought her bed; great, therefore, was his surprise when he passed by the drawing room door and found the candles still burning and his wife nodding on the sofa.

" 'elen?" he called softly, advancing tentatively into the room.

Her eyes fluttered open at once, and she rose from the sofa to cross the room on winged feet. "Ethan! You've come home!"

"Did you think I wouldn't, love?" he asked, receiving her in a warm embrace.

"I — I didn't know," she confessed. "We've never quarreled before. Oh, darling, I'm so sorry —"

Mr. Brundy smothered her apology with a kiss. "You've got nothing to be sorry for, 'elen. I'm the one 'oo's sorry."

"But I said you were selfish —"

"And right you were, at that. I want you all to meself."

"But Ethan, what about Miss Crump? I should feel so dreadful if she were truly your sister, and we cast her off."

"If you want 'er to stay, 'elen, she can stay. Only promise me you'll not introduce 'er as me sister until it's proven as fact."

"Very well, I shall introduce her as my protégée," promised Lady Helen. "Oh, Ethan! You are truly the best of men!"

"I know," he said immodestly, putting an arm about her waist and steering her toward the stairs. "But tell me again."

Lady Helen was happy to oblige, and side by side they slowly mounted the stairs, billing and cooing like the newly married couple they were. When they reached the first floor, however, Mr. Brundy watched in bewilderment as his wife paused before a door at the top of the stairs.

"Where are you going, love?"

"This is my bedchamber," she pointed out.

He gave her a knowing grin. "You 'aven't slept in that room in a month!"

"Then perhaps it is time I did," she replied, turning aside to open the door.

She would have entered, but he blocked her way by the simple expedient of placing his arm across the opening.

"Not a chance, love," he said firmly. "For the first month of our marriage, you called me 'Mr. Brundy' and kept a chair wedged 'neath your doorknob. I've not come this far only to back down now."

Lady Helen colored rosily. "Ethan, we have a guest in the house!"

"And if she's truly me sister," he said,

turning Lady Helen's argument against her with Machiavellian efficiency, "she won't understand the Quality's custom of keeping separate bedchambers. Nor do I understand it meself, for that matter, given the importance you people place on producing heirs. 'Tis a wonder to me that the lot of you didn't die out years ago."

"That is beside the point, Ethan," chided his adoring wife. "Now that we are no longer alone in the house, we must behave with more decorum."

"Must we?" whimpered her sorely tried spouse.

"Ethan —"

"All right, all right," conceded Mr. Brundy, who knew a lost cause when he saw one. "If you want to move back into your own room while the girl is 'ere, I'll not say you nay — only promise me you'll not put a chair under the doorknob."

Lady Helen reached up to caress her husband's cheek. "Thank you, Ethan."

Long after she disappeared into her room, Mr. Brundy stood in the corridor, glaring at the paneled wooden barricade that separated him from his bride.

"Aubrey," he said aloud, "I 'ope you know what you're doing!"

# 4

"Throw yourself into a coach," said he.
"Come down and make my house your inn."
EDMUND BURKE, *Burke's Life*

Mr. Brundy and his ladies accomplished the fifty-mile journey to Brighton in five and a half hours. Their baggage followed at a more modest pace in a second carriage bearing Mr. Brundy's valet, Lady Helen's abigail (who was also to serve Miss Crump in that capacity), the butler Evers, and Cook, lesser servants having been hired from amongst the locals by Mr. Brundy's man of business.

To Polly, accustomed to the rigors of the common stage, traveling in a private post-chaise was an unparalleled luxury, diminished only slightly by the man glowering at her from the rear-facing seat. So well-sprung was the vehicle that, when it at last lurched to a stop in the Marine Parade, she felt none of the stiffness usually resulting from a journey of such length, but fairly bounded out of the carriage to find herself standing before a tall, narrow house with a fine view of the sea.

"What a charming little house!" exclaimed Lady Helen, leading the awestruck Polly to wonder how a charming *large* house might have appeared.

The first evening was spent settling themselves comfortably into the abode which was to be their home until the end of September. When the coach carrying their baggage arrived, Lady Helen was distressed to discover that Polly's entire wardrobe consisted of three drab-colored stuff gowns, two sets of undergarments, a single pair of gloves, a shawl, a bonnet, and a heavy cloak. That evening, she informed her husband that she intended to take Miss Crump to a modiste and provide her with a suitable wardrobe for a young lady making her *entrée* into Society.

"What fun it will be, launching Polly, chaperoning her to assemblies at the Castle Inn or the Old Ship Hotel, perhaps even the Pavilion —"

"Aye, you look like a chaperone," scoffed Mr. Brundy, regarding his wife with fond amusement. "You're 'ardly older than she is!"

"True, but I am a married woman," pointed out Lady Helen.

"You'd 'ave an 'ard time proving it by me," muttered her husband. "But if you've a fancy to play Society matron, love, I wouldn't be averse to giving you daughters," he added hopefully.

"Really, Ethan, I am quite serious!"

"You think I'm not?"

Lady Helen ignored this interruption. "We've scarcely known her twenty-four hours, but already Polly is like the sister I never had."

"Funny you should say that. She's the sister *I* never 'ad, either."

A reproachful look was the only answer he received.

The next day Lady Helen and her protégée descended upon Brighton in force. During the long carriage ride Lady Helen had discovered Polly's fondness for reading, and accordingly their first stop was Donaldson's library. Here Polly was amazed when her noble mentor took out a subscription without even bothering to inquire as to the cost, surrendering one guinea each for membership without so much as batting an eye.

But even this demonstration of Lady Helen's largesse was quickly eclipsed, for when they arrived at Madame Franchot's fashionable establishment in the Lanes, she gave Madame a free hand. Polly's head swam as the birdlike Frenchwoman darted from one gown to the next, extolling the virtues of a jaconet muslin walking dress in a delightful shade of peach that emphasized Miss's creamy complexion, an ivory-colored ball gown whose deceptively simple cut would give *la petite mademoiselle* the illusion of height, and a blue satin evening dress with a beaded bodice which was sure to become all the rage. To all this bounty were added slippers, gloves, bonnets, and fans, until at last Polly felt compelled to protest.

"Surely I cannot need all these things for a three-month stay in Brighton!"

"To be sure, you will need much more," concurred Lady Helen, "but these should suffice, at least for the nonce."

Polly, recalling what tidbits Lady Farriday had let fall, was uneasy for Lady Helen's sake, wondering how her husband might react to such lavish spending. But she did not wish to appear ungrateful, and indeed she would have been less than female were she not delighted at the prospect of wearing such lovely gowns.

Still, until that moment she had not considered that her scheme might hurt anyone, beyond relieving Mr. Brundy of a few shillings which would seem to him as little more than pocket change. Certainly she had never expected her invasion of Society to constitute a major expenditure on the part of her hostess; but then, she knew so little of Society that her ignorance was perhaps not to be wondered at. She tried to cheer herself with the reflection that she was surely closer than ever before to finding her father, who would no doubt be so thankful to be reunited with his long-lost daughter that he would gladly repay Mr. Brundy every farthing spent on her behalf. Nevertheless, she listened to Lady Helen's plans with a heaviness in her heart which had not been there before.

While Mr. Brundy and his ladies wended their way southward to Brighton, Sir Aubrey paid a call on his mother at her residence in Belgrave Square. Dispensing with the formality of being announced, he mounted the stairs with the ease of long familiarity, and found Lady Tabor in the chamber which she referred to as the Wedgwood room. She could not have chosen a more felicitous setting, for Lady Tabor had inherited the fine bone structure and prematurely snow-white hair of her Inglewood forebears, and the pale blue and white color scheme of the room, taken from the china after which it was named, might have been designed to enhance these features.

"You're looking well, Mama," said her son, bowing over her beringed fingers. "I trust I find you in good health."

Lady Tabor gave a languishing sigh. "I daresay I am as well as might be expected for one whose only son seems determined to drive her to an early grave. I have been suffering the most distressing palpitations of the heart."

"For which I am responsible, I have no doubt," put in Sir Aubrey, undisturbed. For as long as he could remember, his mother had enjoyed all the vagaries of ill health while suffering none of its more incapacitating drawbacks. Privately, he was convinced his mother would probably outlive not only himself, but all four of his older sisters. "Tell me, Mama, of what filial cruelty am I guilty this time?"

"Lady Jane Cunningham is to marry Dunstan. 'Tis in the *Morning Post*. Here, you may see for yourself," added Lady Tabor, thrusting the newspaper at her errant offspring. "You might have had Lady Jane any time these past two years, had you made the slightest push to fix her interest!"

"I know — which is precisely why I studiously avoided making any such push," replied sir Aubrey, unrepentant. "But do cheer up, Mama. I shall not be around to vex you much longer."

"Whatever do you mean, Aubrey?"

"Only that I plan to remove to Brighton for the summer. I would not do so, however, without first calling to take my leave of you, ma'am."

"Which can only mean you have wagered far too much on some horse to win the Brighton Cup," observed Lady Tabor in tones markedly similar to the drawl her son sometimes affected.

"Truth to tell, Mama, I was not thinking of horses. In fact, the filly which lures me to Brighton is one of the two-legged variety."

As Lady Tabor wanted nothing more than for her son to marry an eligible young lady and set up his nursery, Sir Aubrey could not have found a surer way to gain his mother's attention. "A girl, Aubrey? Who is she?"

"Do you know, I don't think I ever heard it," exclaimed Sir Aubrey, much struck. "Indeed, I don't think he ever mentioned a name."

"Who on earth is 'he'?" demanded Lady Tabor impatiently. "We were discussing a young lady!"

"No , I think not. A female, unquestionably, but I very much doubt she is a lady."

"Aubrey —" growled his mother.

"She is, or says she is, Ethan Brundy's sister."

"Another weaver? Good heavens! How many of them are going to be foisted upon good society?"

"Only one, I trust. Ethan seems quite convinced the girl is a fraud. I've a fancy to help him get to the bottom of things."

"You would do better to look about you for an eligible female!"

"As I recall, the last time I went to Brighton, I did precisely that — only to have you ring a peal over my head," recalled Sir Aubrey reminiscently.

"I did not mean you were to ogle seabathers through a spyglass!" retorted his fond parent. "Do you know, Aubrey, I'm thinking it has been a long time since I have been to Brighton."

Sir Aubrey's handsome face froze in an expression of horror. "Mama, you don't mean —"

"Precisely. I am persuaded the sea air would do wonders for my poor heart."

None of the many arguments put forth by her son had the least effect in dislodging this conviction from Lady Tabor's mind, and in the end Sir Aubrey was obliged not only to delay his departure in order to give his mama time to prepare for the journey, but also to give up the bachelor lodgings he had hired for his stay, and to post a letter to a Brighton solicitor instructing him to hire on Sir Aubrey's behalf a house suitable for himself and his mother.

Although the delay was no longer than three days, so severely did it try Sir Aubrey's patience that it might have been as many weeks. He was bored with London society, and although he would never have admitted it, even to himself, more than a little lonely. The marriages of both his chief cronies within two months of each other had left the sole remaining bachelor of the trio very much to his own devices, as Lord David had not yet returned from his wedding trip and Mr. Brundy demonstrated a marked preference for the company of his wife over that of the gentleman who had first made her known to him. Mr. Brundy might well wish his fraudulent sister at Jericho, but for Sir Aubrey, her unexpected appearance held the promise of a greater diversion than any he had enjoyed since the day he had prevailed upon Lord David Markham to introduce the parvenu weaver to the Duke of Reddington's haughty daughter. His interest had been piqued the evening Mr. Brundy had first told him of the mystery lady's arrival, and so powerfully did the three-day postponement work upon his curiosity that by the time he and his mama set out for Brighton, the unmasking of the fair intruder was well on the way to becoming an obsession.

Polly's initial visit to the modiste was of necessity followed by several additional visits, during which she was fitted for the gowns which were by this time in various stages of production. On each of these occasions she was accompanied by Lady Helen, a circumstance which meant that Mr. Brundy was, more often than not, left to his own devices. For a man on his honeymoon, he reflected, he seemed to be spending an inordinate amount of his time alone. On the fourth day after their arrival, he whiled away the afternoon by strolling along the shore. This was not the peaceful pastime it might have been, for each time he scanned the watery horizon in the distance, he was reminded of his friend Lord David Markham on the other side of the Channel, enjoying the pleasures of Paris with his bride in blissful solitude. Mr.

Brundy stooped to pick up a handful of pebbles from the sand, and hurled them one by one into the surf in a gesture replete with helpless frustration.

He returned to the house a short time later to discover that visitors had called in his absence. They had elected to await his return, Evers informed him, and were even now ensconced in the drawing room. Mr. Brundy went straightway to this chamber and discovered Sir Aubrey pacing the floor in some agitation of spirits, while his mama perched rigidly on the edge of a low-backed sofa.

"Aubrey! And Lady Tabor. An unexpected pleasure, ma'am," said Mr. Brundy, making his bow to her ladyship.

Alas, Lady Farriday had spoken truly when she intimated Lady Tabor's disapproval of her son's friend. "I must tell you, sir, that I take no pleasure in the company of weavers," replied Sir Aubrey's mama with alarming candor.

Nor had her son any time to waste on pleasantries. "I say, Ethan, 'tis the damnedest thing — begging your pardon, Mama," he added, anticipating his mother's recommendation that he modify his language in the presence of ladies. "There isn't a house to be hired in all of Brighton!"

"If you waited until now to inquire, I don't doubt it," said Mr. Brundy, albeit not without sympathy.

"Not at all!" protested his friend. "I had arranged lodgings for myself, but you can hardly expect me to put Mama up in a bachelor flat. The fact of the matter is, if you want my help with this sister of yours, I must ask you to put us up for awhile."

Mr. Brundy had the sinking feeling that his honeymoon cottage was assuming all the more disagreeable characteristics of a posting house. "Is it as bad as all that?" he protested with a note of desperation in his voice.

"Believe me, Mr. Brundy," asserted Lady Tabor, "only the direst of circumstances could compel me to entreat your hospitality!"

"Believe me, madam, only the direst of circumstances could compel me to insult you by offering it," replied the weaver, making her ladyship an elaborate bow.

Lady Tabor, to whom rank and age afforded the luxury of rudeness, was rarely answered in kind, and her son, confident of his friend's ability to hold his ground, watched in amused expectation for the fireworks which were sure to follow. But he never even heard his mother's reply (if, in

71

fact, reply she made at all), for at that moment Lady Helen returned from her shopping expedition, bearing with her the plague from which he was expected to deliver the Brundy domicile.

She was surprisingly small, as plagues go, with a trim figure swathed in peach-colored jaconet muslin. She had not yet put off her hat, and this confection, wide-brimmed in the gypsy style and tied under the chin with peach-colored ribbons, framed a heart-shaped face with wide blue eyes, a perfect bow of a mouth, and a mass of riotous red-gold curls. Sir Aubrey raised his quizzing-glass, the better to survey his adversary, but he quite forgot the promised scowl. Mr. Brundy had certainly understated the case when he described his uninvited guest as "pretty enough," but in all else it seemed he was quite correct in his assessment. Glancing from the delicate beauty in peach to his friend's rough-edged vitality, Sir Aubrey was quite certain they had never occupied the same womb. The girl was unquestionably a fraud.

"Why, Sir Aubrey, I had no idea you were in Brighton," Lady Helen's voice intruded upon his thoughts. "And you have brought your mama! Good afternoon, Lady Tabor. May I present Miss Crump?"

"Enchanted," drawled Sir Aubrey, making his bow.

"Lady Helen, my doltish son has driven me to Brighton only to inform me that we have no place to stay," Lady Tabor informed her without preamble. "I hope we may prevail upon you and your husband to take us in."

Lady Helen glanced at her husband for assistance, but received only an expressive shrug.

"I — of course, we should be delighted, my lady," faltered Lady Helen. "Unfortunately, we have only three bedrooms, and —"

"Only three?" Lady Tabor bent a disapproving glare on her host. "I should have thought that a man of your means, Mr. Brundy, would have hired a larger house."

"I didn't expect to 'ave 'ouseguests," was his satiric reply.

"There, there, my lady, I am sure we can manage," Lady Helen said briskly. "You, of course, must have a room of your own. Sir Aubrey may share Mr. Brundy's room, and I will share with Miss Cr—"

"Oh, no, you will not!" declared Mr. Brundy in a tone which brooked no argument. "The 'ouse may be full, 'elen, but this is still me 'oneymoon, and I'll be 'anged if I'll spend it with 'im!" he concluded, jerking a contemptuous thumb in Sir Aubrey's direction.

Lady Helen blushed to the roots of her hair. "Ethan!" she cried, aghast. "What will Lady Tabor think?"

"She already 'as the poorest opinion of me, so she can 'ardly think worse than she did before," he said briskly. "Aubrey can 'ave a room of 'is own, and Lady Tabor can put up with Miss Crump. And anyone 'oo doesn't like the room assignments," he added to the group at large, "is welcome to make other arrangements."

As Lady Tabor was not accustomed to being dictated to, and certainly not by anyone of so humble a station as Mr. Brundy, it was doubtful she could have articulated a protest, even had she made the attempt. As for Sir Aubrey and Polly, they were hardly aware of the quarrel in their midst, being fully occupied in taking one another's measure.

"Tell me, Miss Crump, how do you find Brighton?" asked Sir Aubrey, all the while looking her up and down in a manner designed to put her out of countenance.

"Oh, very much to my liking," she assured him. "But will you not call me Polly, sir?"

"No, I will not," he informed her. "For one thing, we are not nearly well enough acquainted for me to take such a liberty, and for another, I doubt I could bring myself to call you such even if we were. It smacks of the servants' quarters, Miss Crump. Should anyone be so bold as to inquire, you must tell them it is a diminutive of Apollonia."

The impostor's blue eyes sparkled with indignation and, had she but known it, her rounded bosom rose and fell enticingly against her jaconet muslin bodice. "Well! Of all the insufferable —"

"What is the matter, Miss Crump? Have you moral scruples against assuming a name that is none of your own?"

Polly stifled a startled gasp. Her first fear, upon being presented to the fashionable gentleman from the bookstore, was that Sir Aubrey might recognize her. Now, however, she discovered a more pressing concern. Clearly, he was in Mr. Brundy's confidence — she really must remember to think of him as Ethan — and was every bit as skeptical of her story as her supposed brother was. Somehow she found Sir Aubrey's veiled hints twice as threatening as Mr. Brundy's more forthright animosity.

"I daresay any person of convictions

would cavil at telling deliberate falsehoods, sir," Polly said, choosing her words with caution.

"One would certainly hope so," agreed Sir Aubrey.

It was perhaps best that Lady Helen interrupted at this juncture, although the news she brought Polly was far from welcome.

"Miss Crump, Sir Aubrey and his mother will be staying with us a few days while they locate a house of their own," said Lady Helen. "I hope you will not object to sharing your room with Lady Tabor."

In the face of Lady Helen's overwhelming generosity to her, Polly could hardly refuse so reasonable a request, and so expressed her delight at the prospect of so exalted a roommate. The three ladies of the party then set out to see Lady Tabor settled comfortably, leaving the two gentlemen behind.

"Well, Aubrey?" asked Mr. Brundy as soon as they were alone. "What do you think of me sister?"

With great deliberation, Sir Aubrey studied the door through which Miss Crump had passed, as if searching for some clue she might have left behind.

"Having never met your sister, Ethan, I'm sure I couldn't say."

Mr. Brundy picked up a decanter from a small table beside the door, and poured a glass of sherry for his houseguest. "Then you agree she's a fraud," he said, pleased to have his own convictions seconded.

"Unquestionably — although a remarkably attractive one," Sir Aubrey added, taking the glass Mr. Brundy offered. "You've been holding out on me, Ethan. The girl is an Incomparable!"

But Mr. Brundy was unimpressed with Miss Crump's charms. "Never mind that! Can you get rid of 'er?"

"I'll do my best, but it won't be easy. She may well take the *ton* by storm. By summer, the *beau monde* is so bored with its own company that any new face, particularly a pretty one, is always a welcome diversion."

"Aye, but they're a fickle lot," pointed out Mr. Brundy, who possessed the advantage of an outsider's objectivity. "Tomorrow they may well turn on the one they dote upon today."

"Too true, my friend. Here's hoping Miss Crump's reign may be a short one," he said, lifting his glass.

"One other thing, Aubrey. Whatever the

reason, 'elen's taken quite a liking to the girl. I should 'ate for me wife to be 'urt."

"Very well. Lady 'elen shall not be 'urt." Sir Aubrey frowned over this declaration, then tried it again. "That is, Lady *Helen* shall not be *hurt*. You know, Ethan, my mother is quite right. You really are the most abominable influence!"

## 5

DALILA: In argument with men
a woman ever
Goes by the worse, whatever be her cause.
SAMSON: For want of words, no doubt,
or lack of breath!
JOHN MILTON, *Samson Agonistes*

Lady Tabor, wearied from her journey, elected to retire early, and so by the time Polly joined her in their shared bedchamber the elder lady, wearing a short jacket of quilted satin over her nightdress, was seated upright in the bed, leaning back against the pillows and reading a book by the light of a candle on the bedside table.

"Oh!" cried Polly, spying the slim, leather-bound volume. "You like to read, too?"

Lady Tabor had not forgotten her son's suspicions concerning Miss Crump, but Polly's enthusiasm for her own favorite pastime could not but gratify, and she bent a thin smile upon the girl. "Since my children have all grown up, I find my greatest pleasure in the pages of a book. Tell me, Miss Crump, have you read *The Lost Heir*?"

Polly's heart leaped into her throat as she recognized the title of the book which had spawned her desperate, and thus far unprofitable, search for her father. She found Sir Aubrey's suspicions disconcerting enough without adding those of his mother. Granted, it was unlikely that Lady Tabor would draw uncomfortable conclusions from the plot of *The Lost Heir*, but if her ladyship were to engage Polly in a discussion of that thrilling work, who knew what secrets her guilty conscience might let slip?

"Yes, I — no, I haven't," she stammered.

One of Lady Tabor's delicately arched eyebrows lifted in mild surprise. "Have you read it, or not?"

"I — I started to once, but I couldn't bring myself to finish it," Polly finished weakly.

"You did not find it interesting?"

"I found the plot so contrived," explained Polly, improvising rapidly. "Surely it is unlikely that Leandro's father would recognize him on sight, having not seen him since he was an infant. Such things don't happen in real life," she added wistfully.

"Of course not!" Lady Tabor replied briskly. "If they did, why should one bother reading about them?"

"Why, indeed?" Polly wondered aloud.

Two doors down, in the largest of the three bedrooms, Lady Helen had prepared for bed and was seated at her dressing table brushing her honey-colored hair when the door opened to admit her husband, who had taken a drop of brandy with Sir Aubrey before retiring for the night. As he discarded his coat, waistcoat, and cravat, Lady Helen broached the subject which had been weighing on her mind ever since Mr. Brundy had dictated the sleeping arrangements earlier that afternoon.

"Ethan, have you noticed anything wrong with this bed?" she asked as he sat down on the edge to remove his boots.

"Only that it's been much too empty of late," he replied. "I must say, Lady Tabor 'as 'er uses. It's worth putting up with 'er to 'ave you back in me bed, love."

She put down her hairbrush and rose from the dressing table, whereupon Mr. Brundy took her hand and pulled her onto his lap.

"Ethan, darling, you should be aware that this bed —"

"Yes, love?" he asked, nibbling at her earlobe. "What about it?"

"Oh, please don't do that!"

"And 'ere I thought you liked it," he murmured into her ear.

"You know I do, but I find it impossible to — to carry on a rational conversation when you — when you —"

"Why else would I be doing it, love?"

"But Ethan, the bed — it — it creaks! Quite — quite loudly, in fact. I was in the room next door, and I could — oh, my! — I could hear it every time you — every time you rolled over, and — and — oh, dear!"

For quite some time thereafter, there was no sound at all, save for the creak-creak of the bed frame.

Floating blissfully in that netherworld between waking and sleep, Mr. Brundy rolled over and reached for his wife, but found only rumpled sheets. Since he was usually the earlier riser of the two, her absence was enough to dispel the last vestiges of sleep, and he opened his eyes to discover Lady Helen already dressed and seated at her dressing table, putting up her hair with deft fingers.

"Up so early, love?" he asked. "What's the 'urry?"

"I intend to be finished with breakfast

and out of the house before Sir Aubrey comes down," she informed him, studiously avoiding the sight of his rumpled dark curls and bristly jaw.

"For 'eaven's sake, why? What do you 'ave against Aubrey?"

She whirled about to fix her husband with an accusing glare. "Ethan, he is in the next room! I tried to warn you that the bed creaks, but you — you seduced me!"

Her unrepentant spouse merely grinned at her. "I 'eard no complaints last night."

"Don't you understand? He *heard!*" Turning back to her looking glass, she buried her face in her hands. "I am so mortified! I'm sure I shall never be able to look him in the face again! How will we explain all that creaking?"

Mr. Brundy considered the matter, then offered a suggestion. "Mice?"

Lady Helen lowered her hands and regarded him with green eyes ominously narrowed. "Go ahead, laugh! I daresay you find the whole thing vastly amusing!"

"No, I don't see anything amusing about 'aving an audience on me 'oneymoon," he retorted. Seeing his bride was unconvinced, he tried a different tack. "You're right, 'elen. Let's not go down to breakfast. In fact, let's 'ave our meals brought up to our room the rest of the day, and let 'em think what they will!"

In two months of marriage, Mr. Brundy had come to know his wife well. The duke's daughter shot a withering glance at her recumbent spouse, then swept from the room with her head held high.

She might have done better to have remained abed, for in spite of rising early, Sir Aubrey had preceded her to the breakfast room, as had Lady Tabor. She murmured a greeting to both mother and son, and after serving herself buttered eggs and toast from the sideboard and pouring steaming coffee from a green and white porcelain coffeepot into a matching cup, she began to breathe easier. To be sure, there was nothing in Sir Aubrey's manner to suggest that he had noticed anything untoward, for he rose at Lady Helen's entrance and obligingly held her chair when she took her place at the table. Alas, her sense of relief was short-lived. Mr. Brundy entered the breakfast room a few minutes later, and although Lady Helen carefully avoided her husband's eye, Sir Aubrey welcomed his host with a bland smile.

"Good morning, Ethan. I trust you had a pleasant evening?"

Mr. Brundy answered in a voice devoid

of emotion. "Quite pleasant, thank you. And you?"

Sir Aubrey shook his head. "Deuced uncomfortable, I'm afraid. I say, Ethan, are you aware of any problem with mice? I was kept awake half the night by a squeaking sound within the wall."

Lady Helen's cup clattered against its saucer, spilling the hot liquid over the gilt rim.

"I don't know as 'ow we 'ave any mice," replied Mr. Brundy, darting a glance at his blushing bride, "although 'elen is convinced there is one rather large rat."

Perhaps fortunately for Lady Helen's composure, Lady Tabor unexpectedly entered the lists. "Good heavens, Mr. Brundy! If you have rodents, send for the ratcatcher by all means, but pray do not discuss the creatures over the breakfast table! And the same goes for you, Aubrey. *You*, at least, have been bred to know what constitutes polite conversation!"

"I beg your pardon, me lady," said Mr. Brundy. "I'll say no more on the subject, except to assure you that I've no need of the ratcatcher. I've a feeling Aubrey won't be troubled by mice again," he added with a wistful look at his wife.

Lady Helen was profoundly grateful

when the company's attention was distracted by the entrance of Polly, dressed for the day in a morning gown of figured muslin.

"Ah, Miss Crump," Sir Aubrey hailed the newcomer. "I trust your rest was undisturbed?"

Polly studied her inquisitor through blue eyes clouded with suspicion. If Sir Aubrey was no less handsome than he had appeared the previous day, neither was he any less dangerous.

"What, pray, would have disturbed it?" she asked warily.

Sir Aubrey gave a negligent shrug and applied himself to the task of spreading marmalade on a slice of toast. "Any number of things: mice — oh, I beg your pardon, Mama! We were not to discuss them, were we? Let me think, what else might disturb a lady's slumber? Indigestion, perhaps, or a guilty conscience —"

"Of what are you accusing me, sir, that it should prevent my sleeping soundly?" inquired Polly in dulcet tones.

Sir Aubrey's expression was all wounded innocence. "Why, nothing, nothing at all! I would no more cast aspersions on the state of your conscience than I would the contents of your stomach — although I must say that if you continue to slather butter all over your bread at that rate, you will find yourself fat as a flawn by middle age."

As Polly stared down at the slice of toast in her hand (which she had unconsciously been covering with butter ever since Sir Aubrey had first begun his interrogation), Lady Tabor again took a hand.

"If this is what passes for gallantry these days, Aubrey, I am thankful to be too old for flirtations! First mice, and now this!"

"As always, Mama, you are quite right. Miss Crump, permit me to redeem myself in my mother's eyes. Your radiant appearance informs me that your repose could not have been other than blissful."

As this declaration was delivered in accents too exaggerated to allow for their being taken at face value, Polly had no illusions as to the speaker's sincerity.

"You are too kind, sir," she responded in like manner. "But any radiance in my appearance must be credited to the beautiful gowns with which Lady Helen has been generous enough to provide me."

"To be sure, Lady Helen has always had exceptional taste," pronounced Lady Tabor.

"Why, thank you," put in Mr. Brundy, bestowing a gratified smile upon the dowager. "And 'ere I was, thinking you didn't like me above 'alf!"

"No doubt her taste in husbands would have been equally nice, had she been at liberty to exercise it," muttered Lady Tabor, glaring at her host.

Silencing her grinning husband with a glance, Lady Helen applied herself to the task of soothing the affronted widow. "Now that Miss Crump has a suitable wardrobe for going about in Society, I have promised to take her to the theater tonight, my lady. Do say you and Sir Aubrey will give us the pleasure of your company!"

"Will *he* be there?" asked her ladyship, and Lady Helen had no trouble identifying her husband as the object of Lady Tabor's inquiry.

"Mr. Brundy will, of course, escort us," she admitted.

Whatever Lady Tabor's retort might have been, it was cut short by her son. "I am sure I speak for my mother when I say we would be delighted to join you," said Sir Aubrey. "But I should be even more delighted, Miss Crump, if you will first do me the honor of going for a drive with me in my phaeton."

For some reason she could not name, Polly found Sir Aubrey's gallantries even more disturbing than his veiled insinuations. Nevertheless, with no less than four people awaiting her answer, she could make only one response.

"Thank you, Sir Aubrey, I should be pleased to go driving with you," she said, then rose to refill her coffee cup at the sideboard.

Sir Aubrey, in the meantime, had turned back to his hostess. "Tell me, Lady Helen, what other plans have you made for Miss Crump's amusement?"

"Well, besides the theater, there are the assemblies, of course — dances, Miss Crump, which I am persuaded you will enjoy above all things! — and perhaps we might have a picnic on the beach one day, weather permitting."

"And have you heard of any masquerades being planned?"

Since masked balls were known to promote licentiousness and a familiarity of manner which was not at all the thing, Lady Helen was more than a little taken aback by Sir Aubrey's query. "Masquerades, Sir Aubrey? None that I am aware of. Why do you ask?"

His shrug was a study in well-bred indolence. "No particular reason. Only that I find masquerades fascinating, do not you,

Miss Crump? No one is what they appear to be."

From her position at the sideboard, Polly bent a sharp look upon Sir Aubrey, but met only a blank gray gaze. "Why, you are in need of more coffee, sir," she exclaimed, seizing upon the excuse offered by his empty cup. "Pray allow me to let you have it."

And so saying, she emptied the contents of the pot onto Sir Aubrey's lap.

By the time Sir Aubrey's groom had fetched the high-perch phaeton, Polly had donned a dark blue spencer and tied the ribbons of a leghorn bonnet over her coppery curls. She had also had ample time to reflect upon her unconscionably rude behavior at the breakfast table. In retrospect, she feared she had perhaps overreacted to an unfortunate but wholly innocent remark. A guilty conscience, indeed!

Sir Aubrey, she noticed, had changed his coffee-soaked buckskin breeches for a pristine pair in a pale buff hue. Still, he made no reference to the circumstances which had made the change necessary, but handed her solicitously up into the phaeton and draped a lap robe across her knees before climbing up onto the seat beside her.

"The wind coming off the sea can be quite chilly, particularly on so cloudy a day as this," he explained, setting the horses at a trot.

Indeed, the day was overcast, turning to gray the choppy waters of the Channel, and Polly, snug and warm beneath the blanket, felt doubly ashamed of having treated Sir Aubrey so shabbily.

"I must apologize again for this morning's mishap, Sir Aubrey," she said, keeping her eyes firmly fixed on his leader's ears. "I cannot imagine how I came to be so clumsy."

"Can you not, Miss Crump?" he asked, turning upon his fair passenger eyes the same color as the waters pounding the cliffs below. "I am sure you fail to do sufficient justice to your powers of invention."

Having been afforded the dubious satisfaction of knowing that her initial reading of his conversation had been the accurate one, Polly had no more regrets for seeking recourse to the coffee pot. "Let us not beat about the bush, Sir Aubrey," she said candidly. "Are you accusing me of telling untruths?"

"Having neglected to provide myself with a change of raiment, Miss Crump, I would not be so bold. Suffice it to say that

I am moved beyond words by your touching reunion with your long-lost brother. One might suppose it to be something out of a fairy story, or a Minerva Press novel — except, of course, that the brother in question balks at welcoming the prodigal."

"For one moved beyond words, you certainly seem to find a great many of them to hurl at me," observed Polly with some asperity. "But one can hardly blame Mr. — my brother for being cautious. After all, he cannot be expected to harbor affection for me when he never knew of my existence."

"But you knew of his?"

Underneath the lap robe, Polly crossed her gloved fingers. "My mother often spoke of him with affection — and regret."

"Regret, Miss Crump?"

Sir Aubrey clearly awaited an answer, and Polly was thankful for having had the forethought to provide herself with a family history before being called upon to answer questions which were likely to prove awkward. To be sure, she would have preferred to make this speech to Mr. Brundy in the presence of his sympathetic wife. Still, she could not deny that there was something strangely exhilerating about matching wits with the obviously suspicious baronet.

"Regret for having given him up," she explained. "You will no doubt think it unnatural for a woman to place her son in the workhouse, but I daresay she was not the first girl to be deceived by a gentleman's promises of marriage."

"Then it appears your mother must have been a very slow learner, Miss Crump. Even if she were very young at the time Ethan was conceived, there are more than half a dozen years separating the two of you. Surely your mother must have gleaned some wisdom in the interim."

"I do not know all the details, for she rarely spoke of her mistake, save for warning me not to repeat it," Polly replied primly.

"And yet, knowing of this supposed brother's existence, you made no effort to find him until now, after he has amassed a fortune, wed a duke's daughter, and established a foothold in Society. Your timing is truly impeccable, Miss Crump."

"I am sure it must appear that way, but it was not until I came to London and, by a happy coincidence, hired a room over a linen-draper's shop that I had word of my brother through his mill. Of course, the fact that he changed his name would have made a deliberate search fruitless, even had I made the attempt earlier."

Sir Aubrey said nothing, but Polly had the distinct impression that he was still unconvinced. "I realize it must sound like a fantastic story, sir, but it is all I have. Alas, I have no solid proof of my claims."

"Nor is there the slightest physical resemblance between you which might lend them weight," Sir Aubrey said with brutal frankness. "Which puts me in mind of another question. How is it, Miss Crump, that you speak like a lady, while your supposed brother has never lost his, shall we say, *distinctive* accent?"

"I cannot account for his speech, since I know so little of his life, but my mother never let me forget that my father was Quality. She was convinced that I should sound like a lady, and to that end, she arranged for me to take elocution lessons from the vicar every Wednesday," Polly explained, thankful to be able to answer truthfully.

As he could find no point on which to discredit her apocryphal tale, Sir Aubrey had to be content to accept it, at least for the nonce, at face value. With a twinge of regret, he tactfully turned the subject, restricting his conversation to the most innocuous of comments regarding the pleasures to be found in Brighton, or the virtues of a high-perch phaeton as opposed to those of a curricle.

Not, he determined with a covert glance at his fair companion, that he had any intention of letting Miss Polly Crump off so easily; if anything, he was more intrigued than ever. He did not for one moment believe her to be telling the truth, and yet he felt a certain grudging admiration for her audacity. She was an enigma, and not at all what he had come to Brighton expecting to find. He had been fully prepared to discover Mr. Brundy's house taken over by a brass-faced high-flyer looking to advance herself in the world. To be sure, no one having seen Miss Crump wield a coffee pot could ever doubt her brass. But Sir Aubrey was forced to admit that he had mistaken the girl's previous profession. Whatever her indiscretions, she was no light-skirt. There was an air of innocence about her that he could not but believe to be genuine.

Innocence. He allowed his mind to dwell momentarily on the word. What a curious adjective to apply to a young woman whom he knew to be lying through her pearly white teeth.

"Thank you for the outing, Sir Aubrey,"

said Polly as he reined in his horses before Mr. Brundy's hired house. "I regret that I cannot say I found it an unqualified pleasure, but I am sure you did your best to make it memorable."

Far from taking offense, Sir Aubrey leaped down to assist her in the task of disembarking. "Since we understand each other so much better than we did before, we shall call it educational, rather than enjoyable," he agreed, bowing over her hand with exaggerated gallantry.

He did not follow her into the house immediately, but lingered at the horses' heads toying with their harnesses as an excuse to watch her retreating form. He found himself looking forward to the evening's theater party with far more eagerness than the occasion warranted. It would be interesting to see what the *ton* would make of Miss Crump, and more interesting still to see how she would maintain her charade under close scrutiny.

"Best call the ratcatcher, Ethan," he murmured under his breath. "I shall get rid of your sister for you, as promised, but I think — yes, I am afraid I must prolong your agony yet awhile."

# 6

Wisest men have erred, and by bad women
been deceived.
JOHN MILTON, *Samson Agonistes*

At eight o'clock that evening, Polly sat before the dressing table while Lady Helen's
dresser performed the final adjustments to
her coiffure. At last satisfied with her handi-
work, the little woman stepped aside, allowing Polly to admire the full effect of
Urling's net over a slip of ivory satin. A
narrow ivory ribbon was threaded through
her red-gold ringlets, and Lady Helen had
insisted upon lending Polly her own pearl
necklet and earrings for the occasion. By the
time she descended the stairs, the former
shopgirl felt very fine indeed.

She joined the others in the drawing
room, and checked in the doorway.
Nothing in Michin's Book Emporium had
prepared her for the sight of so much elegance assembled under one roof. Lady
Tabor, seated in solitary splendor on a
low-backed Grecian sofa, was awe-
inspiring in a black lace gown that empha-

sized her delicate bone structure and snow-white hair. The Brundys, both man and wife, stood near the window with their heads together, Lady Helen breathtakingly lovely in sapphire blue silk, her white bosom adorned with the most magnificent diamond necklace that Polly had ever seen — not, to be sure, that she had seen all that many with which to compare it. Even Mr. Brundy looked surprisingly elegant — or at least he did, until Polly's gaze fell upon Sir Aubrey Tabor. The baronet, dressed in a dark blue long-tailed coat, form-fitting black pantaloons, and a waistcoat of white brocade, quite cast his host into the shade. Polly's heart began to thump uncomfortably against her ribs, and Sir Aubrey, as if hearing the sound it made all the way across the room, chose that moment to glance her way.

"Ah, Miss Crump," he said, his gray eyes gleaming with appreciation as he came forward to greet her. "May I say how much I am looking forward to tonight's performance?"

Although Polly could not but be gratified by the admiration in his eyes, something in the tone of Sir Aubrey's voice suggested that the performance he had in mind was not the professional actors', but her own.

"I, too, am eager to see the play," she replied with the slightest emphasis on the last word.

After the assembled company had finished admiring one another's finery, the party split up, Sir Aubrey escorting his mother in one carriage while Mr. Brundy, his wife, and his "sister" followed in another. The little group reassembled in the box Mr. Brundy had hired over Sir Aubrey's protests, the baronet being loth to let his host bear the entire cost of the Brighton sojourn. But Mr. Brundy had insisted, and as Sir Aubrey was well aware that the weaver could buy him several times over, he capitulated with a good grace. As they assumed their seats, however, Sir Aubrey repaid his friend's generosity by ushering Polly and Lady Tabor to the chairs at the front of the box, leaving Mr. Brundy and his bride to enjoy the privacy afforded by its shadowy recesses.

"It may interest you to know, Miss Crump," said Sir Aubrey, seating himself between his mother and Polly, "that I last attended the theater in the company of your brother. We were at Covent Garden in London, and it was on that occasion that he spotted Lady Helen Radney, as she was then, in a box across the way and

99

vowed to marry her. Within four days, I saw them joined as man and wife."

With an effort, Polly refrained from turning to look over her shoulder at the man under discussion. "I had no idea he was so ruthless," she said, barely suppressing a shudder.

"Ethan, ruthless? I should rather describe him as determined — the only shared characteristic, I might add, that supports your claims of kinship."

"You find me determined, sir?" Polly asked, not quite sure whether to feel flattered or insulted.

"My dear girl, I find you positively obstinate."

Polly was spared the necessity of a reply by the raising of the curtain — a fortuitous circumstance, as Sir Aubrey's pronouncement had rendered her momentarily speechless. She had never been to the theater before, and so was soon able to forget her companion's disturbing remarks in the magical world unfolding on the stage below. Alas, her reprieve was to be a short one, for the first act had not yet ended when Sir Aubrey leaned over to address her in an undervoice.

"I was not aware that you had other acquaintances among the *ton*," he remarked.

"Nor have I, sir," she replied, puzzled by the seeming *non sequitur.*

"You may not know him, but old 'Carrot' Camfield certainly seems to know you," he said, nodding in the direction of a box on the opposite side of the theater.

Gripped by a horrible premonition, Polly scanned the far side of the theater until she located the gentleman to whom Sir Aubrey referred. Her greatest fear since arriving in Brighton was that one of Mr. Minchin's regular customers might recognize her — a fear she acknowledged as largely irrational, since she hardly recognized herself in her elegantly dressed and stylishly coiffed stranger she occasionally glimpsed in the mirror. Nevertheless, she was relieved to discover that the man eyeing her through his quizzing glass was a complete stranger. Her relief was short-lived, however, for the gentleman regarded her with an unwavering gaze which put her quite out of countenance. She could think of no reason for him to do so, for she was quite certain she had never seen him before, much less been formally introduced. He was fifty if he was a day, and his old-fashioned queue, which in his younger days had no doubt provided the inspiration for his sobriquet, had faded to a more muted, albeit undeniably orange, hue. She could not imagine why he should take such an interest in her.

Unless . . .

She allowed her gaze to drift back in his direction, unconsciously twisting one red-gold ringlet around her finger. Yes, he was certainly old enough to be her father, and one might detect a certain resemblance, even from this distance. She wished she might have a closer look at his face, the better to discover what color were his eyes, but although Lady Tabor's opera glasses lay unused on her ladyship's lap, Polly dared not ask to borrow them for the purpose of ogling an unknown gentleman across the theater.

"Who did you say he was?" she asked Sir Aubrey.

"He is styled Lord Camfield, but the earl's intimates call him Carrot — an appellation which, I believe, was even more apt in his younger days than it is now."

An earl, Polly thought. Certainly he would fit her mother's description of a gentleman of Quality. Unfortunately, there was bound to be a certain amount of awkwardness in accosting a stranger and claiming to be his illegitimate child, as well as a number of obstacles to be overcome — his wife, for instance, might be less than pleased to be presented with living proof of her husband's infidelity.

"Is Lord Camfield married?"

The directness of the question momentarily startled Sir Aubrey out of his air of elegant ennui. He subjected Polly to a close scrutiny of which she was blissfully unaware, her attention being fully engaged by the gentleman in the distant box.

"I believe the earl is a widower."

Polly nodded, a gesture indicative of approval which was not lost on the baronet. It appeared the mysterious Miss Crump had not come to find a brother at all, but a husband. Apparently a man more than twice her age would do nicely, so long as he was an earl. Far from being repulsed by such raw ambition, Sir Aubrey marvelled at her effrontery. After all, what was she doing that was not done by every milk-and-water miss ever to darken the threshold of Almack's? The only difference, so far as he could tell, was that she was resorting to trickery and subterfuge to beat the milk-and-water misses at their own game.

But the question remained: why, of all people, had she chosen Mr. Brundy as her "brother"? If a brilliant marriage was what she wanted, surely she should have looked higher than a weaver, even a fabulously wealthy one, to sponsor her in Society. Although now that he thought of it, perhaps she had been less interested in Mr. Brundy's wealth than she was in Lady Helen's social position. In fact, when seen through an adventuress's eyes, the Brundys must appear a perfect combination. Mr. Brundy could fund her little adventure, and Lady Helen could provide the needed social entrée. And if the charade required that she claim to be a near relation, how was Mr. Brundy to deny it? No one, least of all Mr. Brundy himself, knew who his father was, and his mother was too dead to refute the charge. Yes, Miss Crump was a cunning little minx; Sir Aubrey would give long odds to any man for whom she set her cap.

The curtain fell on the first act shortly afterwards, and Sir Aubrey was not in the least surprised when Lord Camfield, with whom he was only casually acquainted, stopped by their box for a visit. As Mr. Brundy and Lady Helen had taken advantage of the brief intermission to take a turn about the lobby (or that was their story, at any rate), Lord Camfield sat down in Mr. Brundy's vacated chair with every appearance of a man preparing to settle in for the night.

"Lady Tabor, your humble servant," said the earl, with a nod for her ladyship. "And Sir Aubrey, always a pleasure. Pray make me known to your charming companion."

"Of course," replied Sir Aubrey, giving Polly a quizzical look. "Miss Crump, may I present Lord Camfield?"

At last face to face with the man who might be her father, Polly searched the earl's countenance for some likeness to her own, and found it in his twinkling blue eyes.

"How do you do?" she asked somewhat breathlessly.

"The better, I am sure, for having met you, Miss Crump," he returned gallantly, raising her gloved hand to his lips. "Tell me, is this your first visit to Brighton?"

"Indeed, it is, my lord."

"And what, pray, do you think of the Royal Pavilion?"

"I'm afraid I cannot say, as I have not had the pleasure of a visit," confessed Polly.

"That will change soon enough," predicted Lord Camfield confidently. "Once Prinny gets a good look at you — but that's neither here nor there. Will I see you at the assembly tomorrow night? It is to be held at the Old Ship Hotel."

Polly nodded. "I believe Lady Helen plans to attend. If so, I will accompany her."

"Good, good! Then I shall hope to have the honor of standing up with you."

"As I never learned to dance, I fear I must decline, my lord. But I'm sure I shall enjoy watching you dance with the other ladies."

Sir Aubrey, catching the wistful note she could not quite suppress, decided to take a hand in the matter. Watching Miss Crump casting her lures for the middle-aged earl promised to be the most interesting amusement Brighton had offered in years, and she could hardly work her charms languishing against the wall. Even adventuresses, he reasoned, needed a helping hand at times.

"We cannot allow you to be dismissed as a wallflower, Miss Crump," he objected. "If you will allow me, I shall endeavor to teach you to dance. Perhaps we can persuade Lady Helen to play the pianoforte for the lessons."

"What an excellent notion!" exclaimed Lady Helen, entering the box at that moment on the arm of her husband. "Depend upon it, you shall be the belle of the ball, waltzing the night away with all the handsomest young men. I assure you, Miss Crump, there is nothing to equal it."

Upon hearing this declaration, Mr. Brundy regarded his wife with a look of unconcealed surprise. "*Nothing,* 'elen?"

"*Nothing,* Mr. Brundy," she replied, glowering at him.

"I am pleased to see that you have such accommodating friends, Miss Crump," said Lord Camfield, with a grateful nod in Lady Helen's direction, "but I must protest this bit about handsome young men. Since Sir Aubrey is to have the pleasure of teaching you to dance, I think it only fair that I should have the privilege of being the first to lead you onto the floor."

Polly agreed to this arrangement quite willingly, and as the curtain rose on the second act Lord Camfield, having achieved his object, took his leave of the party, pressing Polly's fingers in farewell before returning to his own box.

" 'aven't you forgotten something, Aubrey?" asked Mr. Brundy some time later. The theater party had returned to the house on the Marine Parade, and the ladies had sought their beds. Sir Aubrey and his host, however, had retired to the library for brandy.

Sir Aubrey, sprawled comfortably in a leather-upholstered wing chair, idly swirled the amber-colored liquid in his glass. "Forgotten something? No, I don't think so."

"You're supposed to be getting rid of the girl, not playing caper-merchant!"

The look Sir Aubrey bestowed upon him was one of wounded innocence. "I say, Ethan, that's dashed unfeeling of you! Was it not only a month ago that Lady David Markham was teaching *you* to dance?"

"That's different! I was trying to woo me wife away from that bounder Waverly."

"And if Miss Crump expects to snare Camfield, she will need to learn how to go about in Society."

"Oh no, she will not, because she's not going to be around that long! As soon as you can arrange it, she's going back to Covent Garden or wherever it is she came from!"

"Covent Garden?" echoed Sir Aubrey, much struck. "Do you think she's an actress, then? I confess, that thought had not occurred to me."

"I wasn't referring to the theater," Mr. Brundy said darkly.

"No, I am sure you are wrong, Ethan. Your Miss Crump was never anyone's doxy, although the theater might be a possibility, now that I think on it. To be sure, her behavior would seem to indicate that seeing a play was a new experience for her, but I daresay that would be a simple enough matter for any actress worthy of the name."

"I don't care 'oo she is! I just want 'er out of me 'ouse!"

"All in good time, Ethan, all in good time," Sir Aubrey said placidly. "I think your best bet is to marry her off."

"And 'ow am I to do that, I'd like to know? She's got no fortune, and as for family, we don't even know 'oo she is."

"The same might have been said for you, but that didn't stop the Duke from approving your suit," Sir Aubrey reminded him.

"No, and don't think I didn't pay dearly for the privilege!"

"Exactly so. In like manner, a sizeable dowry might inspire suitors to overlook any, er, irregularities concerning Miss Crump's parentage."

"It might," agreed Mr. Brundy, "except for one thing. She 'asn't got one."

"She will if you give it to her."

Mr. Brundy was rendered momentarily speechless, but his thunderous expression spoke volumes.

"Come now, Ethan, if I'm willing to have my toes trod upon, surely you can part with enough for a respectable dowry!" chided Sir Aubrey. "I'll wager Lady Helen spent a tidy enough sum on those togs Miss Crump was wearing tonight. What's a few thousand pounds more to a Croesus like you?"

"I'll not dignify that question with an answer, save to say that me wife's powers of persuasion cast yours into the shade," replied Mr. Brundy.

"Oh, very well, forget the dowry," Sir Aubrey conceded with a sigh. "It will be more of a challenge that way, at any rate. And I must say, the idea of turning a penniless little nobody into the toast of Brighton has its appeal. I haven't had this much amusement since Lord David and I took you under our collective wing."

" 'aven't you, now?" asked Mr. Brundy, his voice heavy with irony.

"Lord, no! There you were, all gauche and unwashed —"

Mr. Brundy took immediate exception to this less than flattering portrayal. "Gauche I may 'ave been, but I was never unwashed!"

"That, my friend, is neither here nor there. The fact is, despite your humble origins, you made a marriage so brilliant that, two months later, the tabbies are still talking about it. Why should not Miss Crump do likewise?"

"All right, Aubrey, marry 'er off, if you will," said Mr. Brundy, resigned to his fate. "And if you can manage to bring the thing off without sending me back to the work'ouse, I'd be much obliged!"

## 7

But oh, she dances such a way!
SIR JOHN SUCKLING, *A Ballad upon
a* Wedding

By the following afternoon, the clouds had given way to rain, turning the choppy waters of the Channel to gray, and leading Lady Tabor to offer it as her opinion that, unless it were to let up very soon, they would not be able to attend the assembly that Friday without their evening slippers being soaked through. As the weather made venturing out of doors undesirable, it was determined that Miss Crump's terpsichoreal instruction should begin that very afternoon. Accordingly, Lady Helen took her place at the pianoforte while her husband and Sir Aubrey pushed the furniture back against the wall to make room for the dancers.

"Really, Mr. Brundy," remarked Lady Tabor, observing this procedure with distaste, "would this task not be better left to a servant?"

In truth, Lady Tabor was less disturbed by the sight of two gentlemen doing physical labor (or, more accurately, one gentleman and one wealthy tradesman thus engaged) than she was put out of temper by the unaccountable disappearance of *The Lost Heir*. She had been quite certain she had left the volume on her bedside table, but when she had gone upstairs to retrieve it, the book was nowhere to be found. She was resolved to have a word with Lady Helen about the moral values of her servants, but in the meantime, she would be forced to look to her host for companionship for the duration of the dancing lesson. While she was resigned to endure the weaver's company with a good grace, it was her sincere hope that Miss Crump would prove to be an adept pupil.

"Aubrey tells me you don't gamble, Mr. Brundy, so I daresay you're no card player," her ladyship observed disapprovingly.

"Not as a general rule, although I've on occasion 'eld me own at piquet," Mr. Brundy admitted modestly.

"You shall give me a partie, then," declared Lady Tabor.

Mr. Brundy conceding to the wishes of his guest, a card table was soon set up before the window, from which point the card players might enjoy the music without interfering with the lesson in progress.

Lady Helen selected a suitable piece and began to play, accenting the first beat of each measure to help Miss Crump grasp the rhythm.

"Your wife is an accomplished young woman, Mr. Brundy," said Lady Tabor. "I cannot imagine the dire straits in which the duke must have found himself, to consent to such a match. I only hope you realize how far she lowered herself in marrying you."

"So long as there are people like you 'oo are kind enough to point it out to me, ma'am, I could 'ardly do otherwise," responded the weaver politely.

"I had four daughters of my own before Aubrey was born, Mr. Brundy, and I must confess it would have grieved me sorely to have given any one of them to a man so far beneath their station," Lady Tabor continued. "Our rank may not be so high or so ancient as your father-in-law's, but Aubrey is related to the marquess of Inglewood on my side, and the baronetcy he holds was one of the first such rank."

"Was it, now?"

"Yes, indeed. Aubrey's ancestor, Sir Reginald Tabor, was created a baronet by King James I in return for services to the Crown."

As Sir Aubrey was not wont to boast of his antecedents, Mr. Brundy was intrigued by Lady Tabor's narrative in spite of himself. "What sort of services, me lady?"

"He contributed a very large sum of money in support of the King's troops in Ulster."

Mr. Brundy's mild interest turned to wicked enjoyment. "Why, Lady Tabor, do you mean to tell me that Aubrey's ancestor *bought* 'imself a title?"

Her ladyship's face assumed an angry flush, and her rigid form fairly quivered with outrage, but if Mr. Brundy noticed these warning signs, he paid no heed to them. "Did you 'ear that, 'elen?" he asked, raising his voice to make himself heard over the lilting notes of the pianoforte and the clipped bark of Sir Aubrey's instructions to his pupil. "Aubrey's great-great-grandpapa bought 'imself a title. Maybe I should do that, too. You'd like to be Lady Brundy, wouldn't you, love?"

Lady Helen never missed a beat. "Not at all," she replied at her haughty best, tossing a disdainful glance over her shoulder at her husband. "I shall not be satisfied with anything less than Her Grace, the Duchess of Brundy."

Even had it not been for Mr. Brundy's

carelessly dropped endearment, Lady Tabor could not have failed to read the message contained in Lady Helen's words, and in that hasty but speaking look.

"Good heavens!" she uttered to her opponent in an undervoice. "Can it be that the most mercenary union in recent memory is in reality a *love match?*"

"Do you find it so surprising that any man would fall in love with Lady 'elen?" demanded Mr. Brundy, with a twinkle in his brown eyes that belied his outraged accents. " 'Tis an insult to me wife, ma'am! If you were a gentleman, I would feel obliged to call you out!"

"And if *you* were a gentleman, I might agree to meet you, if only to silence your impertinence!" retorted her ladyship. "Are you aware, Mr. Brundy, that the whole of London believes you to have bought Lady Helen Radney for one hundred thousand pounds?"

"Aye, that I am — although why they think I would part with such a sum if I weren't already 'ead over ears, I 'aven't the foggiest notion."

"And Lady Helen?" demanded the dowager. "Does she return your, er, affections?"

"As to that, me lady, you'll 'ave to ask

116

me wife," said Mr. Brundy with a smug smile. "Aubrey tells me that a gentleman never boasts of 'is conquests."

Lady Tabor was not the only one confronted with new and unwelcome discoveries. She might have found a kindred spirit in the person of her roommate, who was at that moment submitting warily to Sir Aubrey's instruction. From her first meeting with the baronet, Polly had been aware that he did not believe her to be whom she claimed, and so had been determined to be particularly on her guard whenever she was in his company. One false step, one careless word, might mean exposure and ruin. She could not afford such an ignominious outcome, least of all now, when her goal at last was in sight.

Unfortunately, it was not until Sir Aubrey's arm encircled her waist that she discovered a new and quite possibly greater threat to her well-being. Sir Aubrey's artfully arranged chestnut locks, wasp-waisted coats, and intricately tied cravats might lead one to suppose he was nothing but a dandy, but with a scant twelve inches between his body and hers, Polly was acutely aware of the physical strength beneath the exquisite tailoring. Sir Aubrey's touch evoked a very different response than Mr. Minchin's had done, and Polly, marveling at the new and thrilling sensation, could not but wonder if her mama's downfall had begun so pleasantly. The thought was an unnerving one, and consequently Polly's lithe form grew stiff and unyielding in her partner's arms.

"Good God!" grumbled Sir Aubrey, half dragging his unexpectedly wooden partner through the movements of the waltz. "I've seen men engage Gentleman Jackson in the ring with more grace!"

Polly, stung, trod squarely upon his foot.

As if in accordance with Lady Tabor's wishes, the rain did in fact let up that evening, and by the time the five set out for the Old Ship Hotel on the following night, the ladies of the party had no fears for their slippers. Indeed, at least one of them had no thought to spare for such fripperies in any case, for Polly was beside herself in anticipation of furthering her acquaintance with the man who might be her father. Sir Aubrey, observing the added sparkle in her blue eyes (the effect of which was heightened by the pale blue satin of her gown), thought Mr. Brundy would not be forced to endure his unwanted houseguest's presence much longer; Lord Camfield's bachelor days were surely numbered.

To one accustomed to the elegant ballrooms of London or the exclusive company of Almack's, the assembly room of the Old Ship Hotel must appear nothing out of the common way. Polly, however, had nothing with which to compare it, and consequently was dazzled by the spectacle presented by dozens of richly dressed couples whirling about the dance floor.

True to his word, Lord Camfield hurried forward to claim her first dance. As Polly allowed him to lead her into the crush, she was aware of Sir Aubrey's watchful gaze upon her, and resolved to demonstrate to that exacting taskmaster that she was not so clumsy as he had supposed. Fortunately for the success of this mission, she was relieved to discover that Lord Camfield's embrace left her unafflicted by that self-consciousness which had so hampered her progress under Sir Aubrey's tutelage. In fact, the earl's arm about her waist roused no more unseemly passion than an orphan's very natural joy at being reunited with a long-lost father — an emotion which, though undoubtedly powerful, was certainly more comfortable than that response which Sir Aubrey's nearness had engendered.

"Why, Miss Crump, I can see I have been deceived," Lord Camfield scolded with mock severity. "You told me you could not dance!"

"Nor could I, until Sir Aubrey was good enough to instruct me," insisted Polly. "I am afraid any credit must belong to the teacher, rather than the pupil."

"Nonsense! What makes a good teacher, but an accomplished pupil? I vow you could make any dancing master seem unparalleled in his field."

"You are too kind, my lord," protested Miss Crump, embarrassed by the lavishness of his praise.

Nevertheless, she could not resist glancing toward the wall where she had left her party. Lady Tabor had sought the card room, and Mr. Brundy had claimed Lady Helen for the first dance, but Sir Aubrey lingered beside a large potted plant, leaning negligently against the wall and observing Polly's progress with interest. Their eyes met for the briefest of moments, and he nodded ever so slightly in her direction before the movement of the dance bore her out of his line of vision.

For his part, Sir Aubrey was not a little surprised to see his inept pupil display a grace and ease of movement which he had never suspected she possessed. Her new-found skill brought a smile of cynical amusement to his lips. He might have known the intrepid Miss Crump would rise to the occasion. Whether or not she had ever trod the boards professionally, she was a consummate actress. Surely anyone seeing her tonight for the first time would suppose she was nothing more than what she appeared to be: a young lady enjoying her first dance.

No, she was more than that. Over a long and checkered career, he had seen dozens of young ladies at their first dances, and most of them were simpering little ninnies. Miss Crump might lie like the very devil, but to her endless credit, she had never once simpered, at least not in his presence. And while she might be, as Mr. Brundy had suggested, a scheming little adventuress, she was certainly no ninny. Given a choice between an adventuress and a ninny, he would take the adventuress any day, particularly if she were slender and blue-eyed, with hair that shone in the candlelight like burnished copper. If she were to smile up at him the way she was smiling at Lord Camfield, he might even be tempted to put his own fate to the touch. At this sudden and unexpected thought, his cynical smile faded. Mr. Brundy was quite right. The girl must be gone, and the sooner the better.

"I say, Cousin Aubrey," put in a boyishly high-pitched voice, "who is that absolute angel you came in with?"

Welcoming any distraction from reflections which were becoming disconcertingly personal, Sir Aubrey turned to the speaker, as this personage was prevented by his absurdly high shirt-points from turning to him. The young viscount Sutcliffe, Sir Aubrey's cousin and heir apparent to the marquess of Inglewood, gazed raptly after Miss Crump in a manner indicative of an acute case of calf-love.

"Good evening to you too, Coz," drawled Sir Aubrey. "The angel, as you call her, is Miss Apollonia Crump, a fellow guest in Mr. Brundy's house."

"Oh."

His countenance fell perceptibly, and Sir Aubrey had no difficulty in guessing the source of his woe. Sutcliffe's papa the marquess would be unlikely to countenance any union between his son and a girl with such dubious connections. On the other hand, his cousin Inglewood had always been a starched-up prig. Sir Aubrey elected to take pity on the love-struck youth.

"I believe Miss Crump is a great friend of Lady Helen," he remarked.

"Oh!" Lord Sutcliffe's countenance brightened immediately. "In that case, would you introduce me?"

"The pleasure will be all mine," swore Sir Aubrey. "But if you will take a bit of advice from older and wiser heads —"

"What is it, Cousin?" asked the marquess eagerly.

"As a rule," pronounced the older and wiser head, "angels are vastly overrated. All that virtue tends to pall on one after a while."

"I'm sure Miss Crump could never pall on anyone," declared young Sutcliffe. "Why, a man might spend an eternity just gazing at her!"

Privately, Sir Aubrey suspected that while a stripling might spend an eternity thus agreeably occupied, a man would very shortly require some more active form of adoration. This, however, he forebore to point out to the infatuated young man. The music soon ended, and Lord Camfield led Polly back to the wall, where Mr. Brundy and Lady Helen were also returning.

"Allow me to congratulate you on your pupil's progress, Sir Aubrey," said the earl.

"Miss Crump's accomplishments certainly speak well for her tutor."

"Yes, Miss Crump is full of surprises," agreed Sir Aubrey, smiling down at her. Feeling a tug on his sleeve, he remembered his promise to the love-struck young nobleman. "Miss Crump, allow me to present my cousin, Viscount Sutcliffe. Sutcliffe, Miss Apollonia Crump."

The viscount stammered out an invitation to dance, which Polly, glaring at Sir Aubrey, accepted primarily to put the presumptuous baronet in his place.

All in all, it was an unforgettable evening. Polly danced every dance, and was taken in to supper by Lord Camfield, who asked permission to call on her in Marine Parade the next day. She even had an ode composed to her eyes by a rather disheveled young man whose darkly brooding countenance bespoke his poetic sensibilities. It was not at all a bad night's work for one who scarcely a fortnight ago had toiled behind the counter of Minchin's Book Emporium.

And yet Polly could not consider the evening an unqualified success.

Nonsense, she told herself sharply as she prepared for bed. It was well after midnight, she was tired, and her feet ached abominably. It had nothing, nothing at all, to do with the fact that Sir Aubrey had never once asked his erstwhile pupil to dance.

## 8

O Polly, you might have toyed and kissed,
By keeping men off, you keep them on.
JOHN GAY, *The Beggar's Opera*

True to his word, Lord Camfield called the next day to inquire if Miss Crump might wish to go for a drive. Polly accepted this invitation eagerly, although whether this was due to a desire to further her acquaintance with the man who might be her father or a need to escape the disturbing presence of Sir Aubrey was a question which she preferred not to examine too closely.

"Well!" remarked Lady Helen to the group at large after Polly and her escort had left the house. "What do you make of that? I own, I would prefer to see Miss Crump with a beau nearer her own age."

Mr. Brundy, engaged in reading the newspaper, had no opinion to advance on the subject of Miss Crump and her middle-aged swain, but Lady Tabor had more than enough to make up for the shortfall.

"It is a wise man who takes a wife from

among his own kind," she declared, darting in the direction of her host a disapproving glance which never reached its target, being deflected by the front page of the *Times*. "I hope you, Aubrey, will take a lesson from the mistakes of others."

"Be sure I shall," promised Sir Aubrey from his seat near the window, from which vantage point he could see the earl handing Polly up into his curricle. "I must confess, I have never seen a more ill-assorted pair —"

Lady Tabor nodded approvingly. "Quite right, son!"

"— than Lord Camfield's bays. I wonder what he gave for them? Far too much, I'll wager."

After Polly's departure, Sir Aubrey found himself oddly at loose ends, and so betook himself to Raggett's club, leaving his mother to the tender mercies of her host. The dowager, finding herself alone with the weaver and his wife, announced her intention of visiting first Donaldson's library to search for the first volume of *The Lost Heir*, and then the Lanes for some shopping. She generously invited Lady Helen to accompany her, but that lady graciously declined, being engaged in beading for Miss Crump a reticule which she was determined to finish simply to spite her husband, who had expressed surprise that his wife would endeavor to manufacture with her own hands an item which she might instead have purchased for an exhorbitant sum in any one of thc local shops. No sooner had the door closed behind Lady Tabor than Mr. Brundy cast aside his newspaper and grabbed Lady Helen's hand.

"At last!" he exclaimed. "They've gone! Come on, 'elen!"

"Where are we going?" she asked, reluctantly allowing him to pull her to her feet.

"We're on our 'oneymoon, aren't we?"

"Ethan!" cried his scandalized wife. "In *broad daylight?*"

"When your 'oneymoon cottage turns into a posting 'ouse, me dear, you learn to take whatever you can get. Evers!" he bellowed for the butler as he propelled his wife inexorably toward the stairs. "If anyone should inquire, Lady 'elen is not at 'ome!"

Lady Tabor, meanwhile, paused on the front stoop. It had been exceedingly remiss of her, she decided, not to ask Lady Helen if there were anything she might pick up for her while she was in town. Determined not to be backwards in any attention (for heaven knew the weaver could only benefit from the example set by the Quality), she turned and rapped sharply on the door.

"Evers," she said when it was opened to her, "ask your mistress if there is anything she requires from town."

"Begging your pardon, my lady," Evers replied woodenly, "but her ladyship is not at home."

"What?" demanded the dowager.

"Her ladyship is not at home," reiterated Evers with no small satisfaction. He had not forgotten Lady Tabor's conviction that a member of his staff had stolen her book, and consequently had little love for his master's houseguest.

"Nonsense, man! I just left her in the drawing room. Here, I'll ask her myself!"

Brushing aside the butler's protests, she swept past him and into the drawing room, where she drew up short on the threshold. Mr. Brundy's freshly ironed newspaper lay in a crumpled heap beside his chair, and a multitude of tiny beads littered the carpet, as well as the sofa where Lady Helen had been seated. Of the room's former occupants there was no sign, but from somewhere upstairs, the sound of a door closing shattered the silence.

"Ah, flaming youth!" sighed Lady Tabor,

and beat a strategic retreat.

Polly, freed from the rather crowded confines of the hired house, leaned back against the leather-upholstered seat of Lord Camfield's curricle and lifted her face to the sun, reveling in the feel of the sea breeze on her skin.

"A lovely day for a drive, is it not, Miss Crump?" asked the earl, charmed by the youthful innocence of this gesture.

"Indeed, it is," agreed Polly.

"I am pleased to see you are not too fatigued from last night's festivities," he observed. "If I may say so, you appeared to be quite the belle of the ball."

"Everyone was most kind." Well, *almost* everyone, excepting only certain unnamed baronets who were too high in the instep to dance with anyone so ungainly as herself. She was struck by the sudden thought that an earl's daughter, even an illegitimate one, might not be utterly beneath a baronet's notice.

"Kind?" echoed Lord Camfield. "Nonsense! Enchanted, more like! It is you who are kind, granting the pleasure of your company to one who must seem a veritable Methuselah in your eyes."

"Oh, no!" cried Polly. "I could never

think such a thing of you, sir."

"Still, it would be a rare young lady who did not prefer the company of a beau her own age."

Polly stared fixedly at the gloved hands clutched tightly in her lap. "To be sure, other young ladies might value youth and good looks above all else, my lord, but to one who has never known a father's guidance, wisdom and maturity are no less to be prized."

Thus encouraged, Lord Camfield turned to regard Polly with an earnestness which she found thrilling. "Miss Crump, do you believe in Fate?"

"Fate, my lord?" she echoed breathlessly.

"Fate, destiny, call it what you will," he said with an expansive wave of the hand. "Have you ever seen someone for the first time and known, without a doubt, that your lives were unalterably linked?"

"Oh, yes!" cried Polly, raising glowing eyes to his. He had felt it too! He had recognized her at once, just as Leandro's father had in *The Lost Heir.* "Yes, it was exactly like that!"

Overcome with emotion, Lord Camfield allowed the reins to slip unnoticed from his hand. His spirited horses, unmoved by the touching scene to which they were witnesses, seized the opportunity afforded by their newfound freedom and picked up their paces accordingly, obliging the dazed earl to recall his surroundings.

"This is not the place to speak of such things," he said reluctantly, having regained control of his team, "but I hope to say more on this head very soon."

"I should be pleased to hear it, my lord," said Polly demurely, although her heart sank at the distraction which had delayed the fruition of her hopes.

Still, she must be pleased with her progress thus far. By the time Lord Camfield returned her to Marine Parade, she was resigned to bear with patience the little time remaining before the earl publicly acknowledged her as his own. For now, it was enough to know that *he* knew, and apparently welcomed the knowledge. Consequently, upon entering the house, she greeted her host with civility and her hostess with warmth. If Mr. Brundy's cravat was askew and Lady Helen's hair not so expertly coiffed as usual, Polly's tumultuous thoughts prevented her from taking notice of such trivialities. It was not until she went upstairs to put off her bonnet and pelisse that she recalled Lady Tabor's book, still hidden beneath her mattress. Now that an announcement seemed imminent, she need not fear arousing that astute lady's suspicions. Polly did not recall seeing the dowager below (nor, for that matter, had she seen Sir Aubrey, although she would have vehemently denied any charge that she had looked for him), so she slipped the book from its hiding place and returned it to its proper place. And so it was that, when Lady Tabor returned from Donaldson's Library triumphantly bearing a replacement for the lost volume, she was puzzled to discover her own copy lying on the bedside table, precisely where she had left it.

Marine Parade soon lived up to its name, for following Polly's triumph at the assembly, a veritable cavalcade of young men descended upon Mr. Brundy's hired residence, each bearing a posy of flowers and inquiring of a world-weary Evers if Miss Crump were at home. Although the ubiquitous Lord Camfield was on this occasion absent, his place was amply filled by a pair of captains stationed at the military camp just north of town, a young poet in the Byronic mold, and Sir Aubrey's young cousin, Viscount Sutcliffe.

"I 'ave to 'and it to you, Aubrey," said

Mr. Brundy with some satisfaction, watching from the doorway as his wife dispensed tea and cakes to Miss Crump's court. "At this rate, we'll 'ave 'er wed and off me 'ands in no time."

"Indeed!" muttered Sir Aubrey, less pleased with the sight that met his eyes. "I'll swear, I haven't seen so many useless whelps since I last visited my kennels! I wonder which one she'll have."

"Any one of them may take 'er with me blessing," declared Mr. Brundy with feeling.

"Sutcliffe's expectations are greatest, since he'll be a marquess someday," Sir Aubrey continued as if he had not heard this speech. "Still, I wouldn't advise Miss Crump to entertain hopes in that direction. My cousin Inglewood would sooner cut out his tongue than give his consent to such a match. No, if it's a title she wants, she'd best stick with Camfield."

Far from wearing the willow for the earl, however, Polly was at that moment listening attentively as the poet, Percival Mayhew, read his most recent composition, an ode which, according to its author, had been inspired by Miss Crump's perfection of face and form. Sir Aubrey's lip curled derisively as Mr. Mayhew struck a dramatic stance before the fireplace, his carefully disheveled black locks falling artfully over smoldering dark eyes. His black cravat was tied à la Byron in a large floppy bow, and Sir Aubrey had little doubt that, had there been any way to acquire a clubfoot in imitation of his idol, Mr. Mayhew would have been quick to avail himself of it. Dismissing the poet as being of no importance, Sir Aubrey returned his attention to Miss Crump, and was amused to find that Mr. Mayhew was beginning to lose his audience.

Indeed, by the time the poet had embarked upon his third stanza, Polly had begun to grow weary of hearing herself compared to a naiad, her eyes likened to twin pools, her teeth to pearls, her ears to seashells, and her hair to brilliant tongues of flame — a rather jarring departure from his watery metaphor which was oddly effective, in that it had the happy result of jolting awake his less appreciative listeners.

Her restless gaze began to canvass the room in search of some new distraction, flitting briefly from one guest to another until, as if of its own accord, it settled on the tall, slender figure of Sir Aubrey, leaning negligently against the doorjamb. He met her bored look with one of cynical amusement, whereupon Polly turned her attention back to the poet and schooled her features into an expression of rapt admiration.

That her admiration might be sincere was an idea so ludicrous that Sir Aubrey was able to dismiss it out of hand. He wondered if perhaps she was not quite as certain of Lord Camfield as she would wish. In such a case, he could only suppose her to be keeping all her options open, and silently applauded her forethought. Although Mr. Mayhew lacked the lure of a title, he was possessed of a comfortable fortune; still, if Miss Crump were obliged to spend the rest of her life listening to such twaddle, Sir Aubrey had no doubt she would have earned every farthing.

"I say, Mayhew," cried one of the two captains, when the poet had concluded his opus amid applause which was perhaps more polite than enthusiastic. "It's dashed unfair, the advantage you versifiers have over the rest of us fellows. How, pray, is a soldier to compete? Shall I bring you the head of Bonaparte on a platter, Miss Crump? I shall swim all the way to St. Helena to detach it from his neck, if that is what you wish."

From his vantage point in the doorway,

Sir Aubrey spoke up. "Are we to infer that you see Miss Crump in the role of Salome, Captain? I must protest."

"Indeed, Sir Aubrey?" challenged the captain. "On what grounds?"

"Purely objective ones. Having seen Miss Crump dance, I find it highly unlikely that the sight could inspire any man to perform so reckless a feat as murder."

Young Viscount Sutcliffe, who had been silent up to this point, felt compelled to spring to his idol's defense. "*I* think Miss Crump's dancing is p— *perfect!*"

This pronouncement not unnaturally caused Polly's three other gallants to add their protests to Sutcliffe's, lest they be made to look no-account by a stripling still wet behind the ears. Polly, however, was quite capable of defending herself.

"On the contrary, Sir Aubrey," she retorted. "If my dancing is as objectionable as you imply, there might be a great many gentlemen eager to do away with my dancing master."

"*Touché,* Miss Crump," he said, acknowledging the hit with the slightest twitch of his lips. "I believe the next assembly is to be held at the Castle Inn. If you will do me the honor of saving the first dance for me, I shall endeavor to watch my back."

Whatever response Polly had expected, it certainly was not that.

"I — I should — the pleasure will be all mine, sir," she stammered dazedly.

Mr. Mayhew glowered at the interloper and young Sutcliffe sulked, while one of Polly's military contingent went so far as to reach for the hilt of his sword. Fortunately, cooler heads prevailed.

"Oh, unfair!" cried Bonaparte's would-be decapitator. "Is this how rudeness should be rewarded? Grant Sir Aubrey the first dance if you must, Miss Crump, but promise me the second!"

Even the slowest of Polly's court lost no time in extracting a similar promise, and Sir Aubrey soon had the satisfaction of knowing that his penniless little nobody would not lack for partners. Still, he could not help noticing that, while she promised each of her suitors a dance, she refused to grant the coveted supper dance to any one of them. He cast a speaking glance at Mr. Brundy. If his host were a betting man, Sir Aubrey would give him odds that Miss Crump would go to supper on the earl of Camfield's arm. Really, he thought, someone should warn the chit not to show her hand quite so plainly. She would be better advised to go in to supper with someone else — himself, perhaps. Keeping Lord Camfield guessing would surely guarantee the earl's increased interest.

Polly's retinue remained long past the prescribed quarter-hour deemed proper for morning calls, each gentleman being reluctant to leave his rivals a clear field. Consequently, it was not until Mr. Brundy suggested that her court might wish to assist in Polly's dance lessons by partnering Lady Tabor (while Sir Aubrey, of course, instructed his pupil) that all four gentlemen simultaneously and by fortuitous circumstance recollected urgent business which until that moment had completely escaped their memory.

As Sir Aubrey bade the vanquished quartet adieu, he could not but wonder at Polly's unwavering preference for an earl more than twice her age. To be sure, more than one handsome young man had been rejected in favor of an earl's coronet, but while desire for a title might effectively remove the two captains and Mr. Mayhew from contention, there was still his cousin Sutcliffe to be considered. Already a viscount, Sutcliffe would one day inherit the title of marquess, making his rank higher than Camfield's. And while Sir Aubrey would be the first to admit that the viscount was an idiot, he was objective enough to acknowledge that his cousin's countenance was not ill-favored and might, with maturity, become handsome — a prospect which, one would have thought, would give him a decided advantage over a man with more than half a century in his dish. Or was Camfield's age part of his attraction? If Miss Crump had hopes of soon becoming a wealthy widow, she was in for a long wait; the earl's health was excellent, and there was no reason to suppose he would not live another twenty years or more.

No, there was no accounting for Miss Crump's partiality for Lord Camfield — unless she had truly conceived a *tendre* for him. To be sure, such a possibility defied logic, but it had been his observation that the tender emotion rarely inspired its sufferers to behave logically. Why else would that most pragmatic of men, Ethan Brundy, glimpse Lady Helen Radney across the width of Covent Garden Theater and vow on the spot to wed her? Why, for that matter, would Lady Helen, who had rejected the *ton*'s most eligible bachelors, decide that an illegitimate workhouse brat was the only man with whom she could find happiness? No, crackbrained as the notion seemed, it was the only possible explanation. Miss Crump was in love with the earl of Camfield.

And for some reason, he found that thought more disturbing than the most venal of motives.

## 9

If youth but knew, if old age but could
HENRI ESTIENNE, *Les Prémices*

Sir Aubrey's suspicions that Miss Crump harbored an unlikely *tendre* for her middle-aged admirer were bolstered further on the day of the assembly, when two nosegays were delivered to Polly. As the whole company was present at the time, Sir Aubrey was made privy to Lady Helen's comment that the pink roses from Sutcliffe would add just the right touch to Polly's new gown, which had been delivered from Madame Franchot's shop only that morning. No mention was made of the other suitor, whose offering of violets would have clashed with the turquoise hue of the gown. When Polly descended the stairs that evening wearing not only the much-maligned violets, but a lilac frock which Sir Aubrey would swear she had worn once before already, he formed a very fair estimation of their donor's identity. He made up his mind to put this theory to the test during the promised dance.

"Not to say you don't look fetching,

Miss Crump," he said when the movements of the dance brought them together briefly, "but I fancy myself to be somewhat knowledgeable about these things, and I am quite certain I have seen that gown before."

"That you have," she confessed. "I had a new gown for the occasion, but these lovely violets did not match, and I did so want to wear them."

"You behold me burning with curiosity, Miss Crump. May I be so bold as to ask the name of the gentleman who can inspire any lady to wear the same gown twice?"

"It pleases you to tease me, sir," chided Polly, although her telltale blush betrayed her. "But since you ask, the violets came from Lord Camfield."

"Ah! Taking pity on the aged and infirm, are we?"

Polly's chin came up, all traces of embarrassment flown. "That is no way to speak of one who is your social superior!"

"Superior in age, rank, and all the virtues," agreed Sir Aubrey in a bored drawl, already regretting his rather malicious dig at the earl.

He could not shake the uncomfortable feeling that he had botched it rather badly. He should have known that denigrating

Camfield could only cause a girl of Miss Crump's spirit to defend him. Indeed, if the earl offered for her now, she would very likely accept simply for the satisfaction of putting him, a mere baronet, in his place.

But of course, that was what he wanted. He had come to Brighton for the sole purpose of ridding Mr. Brundy of his unwelcome houseguest, and as far as he could tell, the best way to do that was by marrying her off. If he could expedite the process by driving Miss Crump into the arms of her most likely prospect, why, friendship demanded that he do no less. By the time he surrendered his fair partner to one of her two captains — he could never keep them straight — Sir Aubrey had succeeded in convincing himself that he had accomplished exactly what he intended.

That being the case, he should have been immensely pleased with his efforts when, on the very next day, Lord Camfield called in Marine Parade not to see Miss Crump, but to request a private interview with Mr. Brundy. However, while his host received the earl in his study, Sir Aubrey paced the floor of the drawing room, conscious all the while of a vague feeling of discontent.

It was only natural, he supposed.

Brighton was bound to seem a little flat once Miss Crump had attached her earl, but having fulfilled his obligation to Mr. Brundy, he need not remain there any longer. After depositing his mama in Belgrave Square, he would be free to go wherever he wished and do whatever he pleased. To be sure, London would be dreadfully thin of company, but there were other places he might go for amusement. For instance, he might return to Tabor Hall in preparation for the approaching dove season. This idea, however, was summarily rejected, for Sir Aubrey had a feeling he would very quickly grow bored with his own company. Nor could he visit his Inglewood relations in the North, for the marquess and his son would no doubt remain in Brighton at least until the first week of August and the annual running of the Brighton Cup. He could always see if Lord David Markham and his new wife had returned from their honeymoon in Paris. He doubted they would welcome him any more than had Mr. Brundy and his bride, but at least Lady David, having been married and widowed before, might be rendered less uncomfortable by his presence than was Lady Helen; mice had not troubled his slumber again, just as Mr.

Brundy had predicted. Sir Aubrey grinned. Small wonder Ethan was eager to see the back of them!

Mr. Brundy emerged a short time later to inform Miss Crump that Lord Camfield was desirous of having a word with her.

"Of course," said Polly, and rose to join his lordship with what seemed to Sir Aubrey as unseemly haste.

"Well?" asked Lady Helen breathlessly. "What did he want?"

"What else? 'e wanted permission to ask Miss Crump to marry 'im," Mr. Brundy answered.

"And you gave it to him?" Lady Helen's outraged expression cautioned her husband to answer in the affirmative at his own peril.

"What else could I do?" he asked reasonably. "I've no authority over Miss Crump. She's only a guest in me 'ouse." As Lady Helen opened her mouth to speak, he quickly forestalled the argument he knew was forthcoming. "And don't give me a lot of twaddle about 'er being me sister, because I know it isn't so!"

Lady Helen knew better than to reopen a subject on which her husband's mind was irrevocably made up, but she was by no means satisfied. "Still, you might have hinted him away, pointed out the obvious differences in situation and experience which must doom such a match from the start —"

"I've not seen as 'ow differences in situation and experience 'ave 'urt *us* any," he pointed out.

"But Ethan, he is old enough to be her father!"

"If Miss Crump doesn't want to marry Lord Camfield, she can tell 'im so 'erself," replied her lord and master in a voice which brooked no argument. "I couldn't find it in me 'eart to serve 'is lordship such an ill turn. It 'asn't been that long since I asked the Dook for permission to address you, love, and it's not an experience I'd care to repeat. 'ad me fair shaking in me boots, 'e did."

"Hmph!" muttered Lady Tabor. "Apparently his Grace was not nearly terrifying enough."

"I've no doubt you could teach 'im a thing or two, me lady," conceded Mr. Brundy.

Sir Aubrey said nothing, but concentrated all his efforts on trying not to imagine what might be taking place behind the study door. In truth, his imagination would have been far off the mark. Polly entered the study to find Lord Camfield standing before the fireplace, his hands lightly clasped behind his back. As soon as the door was shut behind her, he came forward to kiss her hand.

"I believe you know why I am here, Miss Crump," he said.

She nodded shyly. "I — I think so."

"My dear Miss Crump — may I call you Apollonia?"

Resentment flared in Polly's breast at Sir Aubrey's intrusion into a touching reunion between father and daughter. Aloud, she said only, "My friends call me Polly."

"Polly," he echoed. "First, I suppose I should tell you a bit of my history, if that would not bore you."

"Oh, no!" Polly cried eagerly. "Not at all!"

"Dearest girl! Very well, then. Being a second son, I never expected to inherit my father's title. After I finished school, I departed for the West Indies, where I managed my father's holdings in Jamaica. I might have remained there indefinitely, had it not been for my elder brother's death in a riding accident. As he died without issue, I became my father's heir, and was summoned accordingly."

As she listened attentively to the earl's

narrative, Polly was struck by the realization that she might have had an uncle.

"Since there were no younger sons, I had a responsibility to marry and produce an heir," Lord Camfield continued. "Not wishing to shirk my duty, I married one of my cousins and fathered both sons and daughters. My wife died seven years ago, and though I was fond of her and mourned her sincerely, there was never that depth of feeling which can exist between a man and a woman."

Polly understood that the earl was trying to explain to her his relationship with her mother — and no doubt to justify it, since he had been married at the time. But although his actions had certainly been very wrong, she was glad to know that he had loved her mother, even if circumstances had prevented him from marrying her.

"Perhaps that feeling was reserved for another lady," she suggested gently.

He smiled, much encouraged by her quick understanding. "Indeed, such has proven to be the case. And now, having done my duty in guaranteeing the succession, I am free to marry to please myself."

Polly's blue eyes opened wide at this unexpected turn in the conversation. She had known that the earl was a widower, but she had not considered that he might wish to marry again. The new countess might be less than pleased to take in the earl's natural daughter, especially if the lady he had chosen was a widow with children of her own to settle. Had she found her father at last, only to lose him again? Her heart plummeted at the thought.

"This — this is news, indeed!" said Polly, trying valiantly for his sake to sound pleased. "I — I wish you very happy, my lord."

"It is my wish that you will *make* me very happy," stated the earl ardently, possessing himself of her hands. "My dear Miss Crump — Polly — will you do me the honor of becoming my wife?"

Polly, tugging to free herself, stared in horror as her father was transformed into a suitor before her very eyes. "You wish to *marry* me?"

"More than anything!" declared Lord Camfield, struggling to reclaim her hands so that he might press moist kisses into her palms.

"Why, it's *indecent!*" Polly exclaimed, snatching her hands away.

"Never say so! You are young, perhaps, but I will teach you to love me," the earl insisted as he caught her about the waist, having abandoned the attempt to recapture her hands.

"But I thought you wanted to *adopt* me!" cried Polly, aghast.

"*Adopt* you?" echoed the earl, his ardor considerably cooled by this revelation. "Surely my attentions have been too marked to be misread!"

"I believed your attentions to be those of a father to his daughter!"

"If that is so, I do apologize, but — *adopt* you, you say? Why would I want to do such a thing?"

"Because you have red hair, of course!" said Polly, as if that explained everything. "And what about those blue eyes? How do you explain *those?*"

Any disappointment Lord Camfield might have felt at the rejection of his suit very quickly turned to heartfelt relief. Clearly the girl was queer in her attic. A pity, too, for she was a pretty little thing, but he could not say he had not been warned. When he had told Mrs. Digby, his nearest neighbor, of his intention to re-marry, she had warned him of the folly of courting a girl so much younger than himself, and now it seemed that she was quite right. A wise woman, Mrs. Digby, and though she had been widowed for nigh on twenty years, she was still handsome. He would pay a call on her on his way home. She would no doubt be pleased to know he had come to his senses, and not a moment too soon.

"Well!" said the earl with great dignity. "I would not press you to accept a suit which I can see is unwelcome. Please accept my best wishes for your future health — er, happiness."

After making an excruciatingly formal bow to Polly, the spurned lover took his leave of the quartet in the drawing room (all of whom were clearly agog with curiosity), demanded his hat and cane of Evers, and took his leave without further ado.

Polly, meanwhile, remained in the study, alone with the wreckage of her hopes and dreams. Blindly, she stared into the fire, until a slight sound from the doorway made her look up. Sir Aubrey stood just inside the door, leaning negligently against the wall.

"Well, Miss Crump," he drawled, "are we to wish you happy?"

It was the last straw. With a sob, Polly ran from the study and up the stairs to the privacy of her own room.

Polly remained in her room for most of

the day, and when she came down to dinner that night the other four members of the household, by mutual consent, restrained themselves from plying her with questions regarding her abortive engagement. When, three days later, her dismals showed no signs of lifting, Lady Helen grew concerned.

"I cannot say I am sorry that Polly spurned the earl's offer," she confided to her husband that night as she sat at the dressing table brushing out her hair. "Still, I hate to see her so blue-deviled. I wish there was something we could do for her."

Mr. Brundy, already stretched out on the bed, looked up hopefully. " 'ow about we send 'er on a long repairing lease?"

"Ethan, do be serious!" scolded Lady Helen.

"You think I'm not?"

Of course he was not, and they both knew it — Lady Helen because almost three months of marriage had taught her that her husband was by far too good-hearted to turn anyone out who was truly in need, and Mr. Brundy because he had his own suspicions regarding Miss Crump. He had voiced these to no one as yet, not even his beloved wife, but there were times when he suspected that if he intended to maintain his friendship with Sir Aubrey, he might as well make the best of Miss Crump. He only wished he might be on hand when Sir Aubrey broke the news to his mama.

"I know!" exclaimed Lady Helen. "We shall have a picnic on the seashore. I don't know why I didn't think of it sooner. That should help coax her out of the dismals, don't you think?"

Receiving no answer, she laid aside her hairbrush and turned to her spouse, prepared to repeat the question. Mr. Brundy lay on his back with his hands clasped behind his head and his eyes closed. As if conscious of the disapproving look being leveled at him, he chose that moment to emit a loud, and patently false, snore. Choking down a most undignified giggle, Lady Helen snatched up a pillow and threw it at his unsuspecting head, whereupon Mr. Brundy, not to be bested, grabbed her by the wrist and pulled her down onto the bed beside him, smothering her laughing protests by the simple expedient of covering her mouth with his own.

Miss Crump was not mentioned again until morning.

# 10

There is a rapture on the lonely shore,
There is society, where none intrudes.
GEORGE NOEL GORDON,
LORD BYRON,
*Childe Harold's Pilgrimage*

A party of four set out for the seashore the following day, Lady Tabor electing to remain indoors and finish *The Lost Heir.* Sir Aubrey, aware that Miss Crump's unbetrothed state meant her continued presence under Mr. Brundy's roof (and disturbed to find himself so pleased by a circumstance which ran so counter to his friend's interests), was resolved to give the newly married pair as much privacy as possible during the outing, and to this purpose volunteered to drive Miss Crump in his own phaeton, leaving Mr. Brundy and his bride to bring up the rear. Unlike the baronet, who had been placed in the saddle almost as soon as he was breeched, Mr. Brundy's knowledge of horses was strictly utilitarian, and consequently he drove at a much more sedate pace. Soon Sir Aubrey and Miss Crump had left them far behind.

Polly, uncomfortable at finding herself alone with him, felt compelled to fill the silence. "How fortunate that it did not rain today! That would have been a shame, after Lady Helen went to so much trouble."

"Rain? Interfering with the plans of Lady Helen Brundy *née* Radney? My dear Miss Crump, no mere cloud would be so bold. Even the sun yields to Lady Helen's wishes."

"Indeed, it would seem so," Polly agreed, although privately she thought it a great pity that Lady Helen's father had not done likewise, and allowed his daughter to marry whom she pleased. On the other hand, if Lady Helen had not been forced into marriage with the wealthy Mr. Brundy, then she, Polly, would have had nowhere to go when she lost her position at Mr. Minchin's shop.

This was an unfortunate observation, as it reminded her of how woefully she had fallen short of her goal. When she had been summoned to the study to see Lord Camfield, she had been sure he was going to tell her he was her father. But marriage! It was indecent. She shuddered at the thought.

"Are you cold, Miss Crump?" asked Sir

Aubrey, observing this involuntary gesture.

"No, not at all, though the wind off the Channel is brisk," she replied.

Spurning the more populated areas where would-be sea bathers were wheeled into the surf by horse-drawn bathing machines, he drove his fair companion to a secluded strip of beach some distance away and drew his horses up to await the Brundys. They had not long to wait and, once reunited, the foursome spread a cloth on the pebble-strewn beach and settled themselves comfortably. The ladies unfurled their sunshades to protect their complexions, while the gentlemen divested themselves of their tailcoats. Having tended to their external comforts, they were free to concentrate on the internal, and feasted on cold chicken, fruit, and cheese from a hamper prepared by the Brundys' cook. When this was finished, Sir Aubrey offered his arm to Polly, and they strolled along the beach.

"It is lovely, isn't it?" asked Polly, gazing out to sea.

"Indeed, it is," agreed Sir Aubrey. "I am surprised you have not brought your sketch pad, Miss Crump. Most young ladies of my acquaintance would feel compelled to commit the scene to paper."

"Perhaps I should have as well, had I ever learned to draw."

"You shock me, Miss Crump. I thought drawing was one of the most basic of female accomplishments."

"I regret to inform you, sir, that I have no accomplishments at all," replied Polly, with a defiant lift to her chin.

"On the contrary. You brought Lord Camfield up to scratch, and that must be judged a considerable accomplishment. I wonder you went to the trouble, though, if you did not intend to have him."

Polly could not allow this veiled accusation to go unchallenged. "I never gave Lord Camfield any reason to think I wished to marry him!" she retorted.

"Did you not, Miss Crump? I beg to differ. It seems to me that when a young lady reserves all the choice dances for a particular gentleman, even plans her wardrobe to coordinate with the flowers he sends, he is justified in believing her to feel a certain partiality for him." Sir Aubrey was both amazed and appalled at the words pouring forth from his own lips. If he had been so pleased to discover that Miss Crump had spurned the earl's offer, why was he now raking her over the coals for that very thing? Knowing instinctively that the question would not bear close scrutiny, he sought refuge in ascribing to her ever more sinister motives. "Unless, of course, you have your heart set on becoming a marchioness, and were merely using Camfield to make young Sutcliffe jealous. That thought, I confess, had not occurred to me until now."

"Then I fear your awe-inspiring powers of deduction are quite wasted on me, Sir Aubrey," she informed him coolly. "It can be none of your business which gentlemen I choose to encourage, or for what purpose."

"As far as Lord Camfield is concerned, that is certainly true, but in the case of Sutcliffe, I am afraid I must disagree. Besides being underage, he is my cousin, and where the reputation and dignity of my family is threatened, I must always deem it my business to interfere, if necessary."

"If you find me so objectionable, sir, I wonder you have not denounced me as an imposter long before now."

"I have wondered that too, Miss Crump," he confessed, regarding her with a curiously unreadable expression in his gray eyes. "More than once, I might add. I daresay it is because I should find Brighton deadly dull without you."

Although their pace was leisurely, Polly's heart began to pound, and her breath came in short, shallow gasps, as if she had run all the way up the beach. "I think we had best turn back, Sir Aubrey," she said with a fair imitation of calm. "You have obviously been in the sun too long. That last sounded suspiciously like a compliment."

"*Touché*, Miss Crump," he acknowledged with a smile. "I fear I am giving you the poorest opinion of me. As I haven't the traditional olive branch to offer, I hope you will accept this instead."

Reaching into the inside pocket of his coat, he withdrew a slender brass cylinder.

"Oh, what is it?" asked Polly, intrigued.

"A spyglass," he answered, extending it to its full length. "They are a very popular item in the local shops, mostly with young bucks hoping for a glimpse of the young ladies entering the water from the bathing machines. Here, have a look."

"I will remember that if Lady Helen ever suggests we try the bathing machines," Polly resolved, raising the glass to her eye and scanning the horizon. "Tell me, Sir Aubrey, has your glass been employed in such a cause?"

"As I offered it to you for the express

purpose of raising your opinion of me, I had best not answer that question."

Polly laughed in spite of herself. "Wicked man," she chided, turning so that she might examine the beach along which they had come. "How much nearer everything looks! There is our picnic cloth, still lying on the ground, and there by the water — oh, my!"

At the edge of the water, standing ankle-deep in the surf, a barefoot Mr. Brundy clasped his wife in his arms and kissed her passionately. More shocking still was the curious behavior of Lady Helen, who had shed her shoes and stockings and with one hand held her skirts clear of the water, exposing her bare legs almost to the knees. The fingers of her other hand were buried in her husband's curly black hair, and she returned his kiss with every appearance of enthusiasm.

Polly jerked the glass downward, her eyes wide with shock and horror.

"What is the matter?" asked Sir Aubrey, taking the spyglass from her nerveless fingers. Raising it to his own eye, he scanned the beach until he located the cause of her distress. "Grossly improper, to be sure, but I daresay such behavior is to be expected in newly married couples when they believe themselves to be unobserved."

"But — but I thought — I was under the impression that theirs was a — a marriage of convenience!"

Now it was Sir Aubrey's turn to be surprised. "Good God! Can you have remained under their roof for all of a month without realizing they are mad for one another?"

"How could I have known? They are so unalike and, except to argue, they seem to have very little to say to each other!"

"No doubt they are busy doing things other than talking," drawled Sir Aubrey. "And if they argue — which, I confess, I had not noticed — it is probably due to the strain of behaving decorously when they are wishing the lot of us at Jericho. You really are *de trop*, my dear," he added, albeit not unkindly.

"If I am, then so too must you be!" she retorted.

"I shan't deny it. Still, there is one telling difference: I am here at Mr. Brundy's invitation."

"I don't believe you! If he were truly in love with his wife, why should he invite you along on his honeymoon?"

"Can you not guess? He hoped that I might be able to rid him of you."

Polly had the sudden and uncomfortable feeling that the ground was crumbling beneath her — a sensation heightened, no doubt, by the sand shifting beneath her feet. She gazed at the watery horizon with unseeing eyes, weighing her ever-dimming prospects against Sir Aubrey's unwelcome revelations.

"I meant no harm, truly I did not," she said at last. " 'Twas only that I had nowhere else to go. I thought, when Lady Farriday said —"

Sir Aubrey leaped on the familiar name. "Lady Farriday? I thought you said you had no other acquaintances among the *ton*."

Polly permitted herself a humorless laugh. "Her ladyship would hardly claim me as an acquaintance. I saw her once in Minchin's Book Emporium. You were there on that occasion, as well."

Sir Aubrey shook his head. "I'm sorry. I'm afraid I don't remember you."

"Nor would I expect you to. I was a shopgirl."

There was no trace of self-pity in her voice, and her chin, though it showed a tendency to quiver, was held at a proud angle which Sir Aubrey found oddly touching. He took her hand and tucked it into the crook of his arm.

"And how did you come to take up residence with the Brundys?" he asked as they continued up the beach.

She was weary of keeping the secret, yet hesitant to confide in him. He could read the struggle plainly in her face, and seeing her glance uncertainly up the beach, he added hastily, "Never fear on their account, Miss Crump. They shan't miss us."

"You think I meant to take advantage of Mr. Brundy and his wife, but such was not my intention," Polly began hesitantly. "I came to London to find my father."

"Who is he?"

"I don't know. I know only that he is a gentleman, and that I bear a marked resemblance to him. When Lord Camfield showed me such — such flattering attention, I thought perhaps I had — but that is neither here nor there. I came to London and obtained a position in Minchin's Book Emporium, in the hopes that I might one day come in contact with my father."

"Did it never occur to you that your plan was, shall we say, a bit simplistic?" Sir Aubrey asked with unwonted gentleness.

"Not at the time," confessed Polly. "And even if it had, I might well have pursued it

164

anyway, for I have always been impulsive to a fault."

"I take it your plans went awry?"

"That would be putting it mildly, I'm afraid. I lost my position in the shop. Mr. Minchin said business had fallen off, and he would have to let me go. And then, in almost the same sentence, he — he made me an indecent offer. I could not find another position, I had no family, and nowhere else to turn but the workhouse. Then, through an astonishing series of circumstances which I could only ascribe to a benevolent Providence, I learned of Mr. Brundy. He also had no father, and he was wealthy enough that it would be no burden on him if I were to be his guest, only until I found my father."

"And yet, knowing it to be false, you claimed to be his sister."

"I daresay it sounds scheming and unscrupulous, but after — what happened — with Mr. Minchin, I felt it wise to protect myself from unwanted overtures."

"Unwanted overtures? From Ethan?" To Polly's chagrin, Sir Aubrey threw back his head and laughed out loud, startling a flock of gulls. They flew away, their mocking cries echoing Sir Aubrey's laughter.

"I am glad you find it so amusing," Polly said stiffly.

"No, no, I beg your pardon," said Sir Aubrey, choking down another fit of mirth. "I am sure your situation must have been most uncomfortable. Had you but known it, your virtue could not have been in safer hands. If ever a man was besotted with his own wife, that man is Ethan Brundy."

"I could hardly have been expected to know that!"

"To be sure, you could not," Sir Aubrey said soothingly.

"And so you have all the satisfaction of knowing that your first assessment of me was correct," Polly said in summary, meeting his gray gaze with one of false bravado. "I am nothing but a scheming adventuress. Now that you know the truth, Sir Aubrey, what do you intend to do with it?"

Here, at last, was all he needed to fulfill his promise to Mr. Brundy. He had only to drop a few words into the right ears, and the so-called Miss Crump would find herself ostracized from polite society. She might as well have handed him the information on a silver platter — and yet he could not bring himself to betray her. He felt, in some indefinable way, responsible for her. It was a new sensation, and a curiously pleasant one.

"I think you should tell Mr. Brundy," he said at last. "As you said, he has no father, and although Ethan is not one to brood, I think he sometimes feels the lack as keenly as you do. I suspect you might find him surprisingly sympathetic."

Polly's face blanched. "No, I could not! Why should he show me any pity when he has every reason to despise me? Pray, don't ask me to do such a thing! Only say nothing, and I will slip away, disappear —"

Sir Aubrey seized her by the shoulders and shook her roughly. "If you dare to do such an idiotish thing, I swear I shall hunt you down and thrash you soundly!" Startled by his own vehemence, he released her somewhat sheepishly and continued on a more moderate note. "Even if you were to disappear, where, pray, would you go? No, having committed yourself this far, you had best stick it out, Miss Crump."

"My mother's name was Hampton," interpolated Polly.

Sir Aubrey dismissed this information with a wave of his long, aristocratic hand. "Crump, Hampton — it matters little, as you seem to change it as often as other women do bonnets. Tell me, what would you say to the idea of marriage?"

Polly's blue eyes opened wide, and her heart, which had seemed so heavy only moments earlier, seemed to sprout wings and take flight. "Marriage?"

"Why not? You haven't the bloodlines for a brilliant match, but you are genteel enough for a respectable one, and besides having a powerful ally in Lady Helen, you are young and, I suppose, pretty enough," he conceded, falling back on Mr. Brundy's unenthusiastic description. "I shouldn't think you would want to spend the rest of your life listening to Mr. Mayhew's atrocious rhyme, but either of your captains should serve the purpose. If you were capable of bringing an earl to the point, a mere captain should be no great hardship. What do you say?"

The wings of Polly's heart were abruptly clipped, and that organ plummeted precipitously back to earth, bypassing its usual locale in order to settle somewhere in the region usually occupied by her stomach. "I shall have to give it some thought," she answered evasively. "And now I think we had best return to Lady Helen and Mr. Brundy."

And as they made their way back up the beach, Polly had the dubious satisfaction of knowing that the one gentleman in all Brighton to whom she could see herself wed was also the one who seemed the most unmoved by her charms.

## 11

What is a kiss? Why, this . . .
ROBERT HERRICK, *Hesperides*

"And just what do people *do* at a rout,
anyway?" Mr. Brundy asked his wife that
evening as he tied his cravat before the
mirror.

"It might be easier to tell you what they
*don't* do," she replied, frowning in concen-
tration into her own mirror as she affixed a
dangling ruby-and-pearl earring to her earlobe. "There will not be dancing or cards,
nor any refreshments. We shall wait in line
for half an hour to greet our host and
hostess, mill about inside for another half
hour, and wait in line yet another half hour
for our carriage to be brought round so
that we may go home."

"I can 'ardly wait," said Mr. Brundy with
a marked lack of enthusiasm, then suggested on a more hopeful note, "What if
you start feeling poorly 'alfway through the
evening? Then we could slip out early."

But this suggestion found no favor with
Lady Helen. "Ethan!" she scolded her

graceless spouse. "That is no way to reward Lord and Lady Belmont's kindness in extending us an invitation."

"It was only a thought," shrugged Mr. Brundy, abandoning it with some regret. "What do we do while we're milling about, as you say?"

"Why, talk, of course!"

"About what?"

"One another, mostly."

Mr. Brundy looked pained. "Tell me again, 'elen. Why are we going?"

"Because rumor has it that the Prince Regent is in residence at the Royal Pavilion, and may make an appearance. It is high time you made your bow to your Sovereign. Here, let me look at you."

Mr. Brundy dutifully turned and presented himself for inspection. As it was his habit to dress for everyday in loosely tailored, comfortable clothing, Lady Helen was always slightly taken aback by the sight of her husband in full evening attire. Although her heart gave a now-familiar little flutter, she gave no outward sign, merely looking him critically up and down before plucking a minuscule speck of lint from his sleeve.

"You'll do," she declared at last, giving a nod of approval.

Still, it was a very nervous Lady Helen who entered Lord and Lady Belmont's summer home on the Steine a short time later on Mr. Brundy's arm. She had been married for almost three months, and during that time had grown increasingly annoyed at seeing the man she loved snubbed by many who were far inferior to him in character. Not even in his own home could he find unqualified acceptance, so long as Lady Tabor remained under his roof; indeed, when that lady was in one of her more disagreeable moods, Lady Helen was hard pressed to hold her tongue. Only the knowledge that her husband would be far more distressed by her attempts to defend him than he was by her ladyship's jibes had kept Lady Helen silent thus far. Indeed, he insisted that Society's scorn bothered him not at all, but Lady Helen (perhaps because at one time she had been among the most scornful) could not dismiss it so cavalierly. If he should find favor with the Prince Regent, however, his position must be assured, for with royal approval, all doors would be opened to him. And if Lady Helen had any doubts as to her base-born husband's ability to comport himself in the presence of royalty, she would never admit to so disloyal a thought, even to herself.

They took their places in the line, along with Polly, Sir Aubrey, and his mother, and after the thirty-minute wait which Lady Helen had predicted, finally found themselves inside. After saying all that was proper to their host and hostess, the little group scattered, Lady Tabor joining a group of her cronies while Polly was quickly claimed by a rapturous Mr. Mayhew. Sir Aubrey was sorely tempted to follow and rescue her, but as he had a fancy to see his friend presented to the Regent, he mastered the temptation and remained with Mr. Brundy and his bride.

That the royal presence was expected was immediately evident, for the windows were all tightly shut and the number of wax candles burning was enough to make the room uncomfortably warm. This, as Lady Helen patiently explained to her husband, was because the Prince Regent had a morbid fear of taking a chill.

"Not a chance of it in 'ere," remarked Mr. Brundy, whose starched shirt-points were already beginning to wilt.

"How true!" commiserated Sir Aubrey, sighing over the once-immaculate cravat which had taken him the better part of an hour to achieve. "But better by far for us humbler mortals to swelter than for His Royal Highness to catch cold. Is that not so, Lady Helen? Lady Helen?"

Lady Helen made no reply, but her face had gone deathly pale, and the Chinese crape fan to which she had sought recourse against the oppressive heat grew still.

" 'elen, love, are you all right?"

As her husband looked on in horror, Lady Helen's eyes rolled back, and her fan slipped from her nerveless fingers. She swayed alarmingly and would have crumpled to the floor in a heap, had Mr. Brundy not caught her against his chest. His initial fear was quickly allayed by the memory of their conversation earlier that evening, when he had suggested that she feign illness so that they might take an early leave. Still, her performance had been chilling in its accuracy.

"Aubrey, 'ave the carriage brought round," he instructed the baronet. "I'm taking me wife 'ome. You'll see to your mum and Miss Crump?"

Sir Aubrey assured him on this head and promptly departed to see to the carriage. Mr. Brundy, rejecting offers of sal volatile and burned feathers from the small crowd which had been attracted by the commotion, lifted his wife's limp body in his arms and bore her from the overheated room. Her eyes fluttered open as he was settling her comfortably in the carriage.

"Good girl!" he said approvingly. "You could've given me some warning, though. Gave me a rare turn, you did!"

"Ethan?" she asked weakly. "What happened?"

"It's all right, we got away clear. I 'ave to 'and it to you, love, I've never felt so unnecessary. You'd no need to wed me for me money, after all. You could've made your fortune at any time on the stage."

"But Ethan, darling, I wasn't acting."

Mr. Brundy stared at his wife, his expressive countenance bearing an arrested look. "You what?"

"I daresay it was due to the heat, or perhaps I got too much sun this afternoon," Lady Helen speculated. "Whatever the cause, for the first time in my life, I fainted!"

While Mr. Brundy bore his bride back to the Marine Parade, Sir Aubrey notified his mama of Lady Helen's indisposition and set out to do the same for Miss Crump. Here he had considerably more difficulty, for that young lady was nowhere in sight. Recalling that he had last seen her in the company of the effusive Mr. Mayhew, Sir Aubrey began to fear the worst, and expanded his search to include not only the larger public rooms, but the more secluded alcoves as well. While passing a pair of French windows opening onto a small balcony, he chanced to glance outside and at last located his quarry, struggling in the arms of Mr. Mayhew.

To Polly, the opportunity to be presented to royalty had quickly turned into a disaster. When Mr. Mayhew had greeted her with such eagerness, she had been only too happy to respond in kind, if only to demonstrate to certain baronets that *some* gentlemen found her desirable. It had not been long before she, like so many other guests, began to feel the effects of the heat, and when Mr. Mayhew suggested that they step outside for a breath of fresh air, she had welcomed this imminently logical suggestion. Unfortunately, it had not been long before this breath of fresh air had turned into an impassioned declaration, and by the time Sir Aubrey glanced out the French windows, the poet had been emboldened to take the fair object of his affections into his arms.

"Mr. Mayhew, I must ask you to desist!" protested Polly, struggling to free herself as her admirer tried to steal a kiss. "Your conduct is most improper!"

The poet, however, was unmoved by this argument. "What has cold propriety to say in the face of passion's demands?"

"At this moment, cold propriety suggests you stop making such a cake of yourself," drawled a bored voice.

Polly and her ardent swain turned as one to discover Sir Aubrey stepping onto the balcony and closing the door behind him.

"Good evening, Mayhew. Your servant, Miss Crump."

Mr. Mayhew, feeling rather foolish, sought refuge in braggadocio. "I beg leave to inform you, sir, that your presence is unwelcome!"

Sir Aubrey favored the poet with a long and quelling look through his quizzing glass, decided he was not worth the effort of a reply, and turned his attention to Polly. "And what of you, Miss Crump? Do you find my presence unwelcome, as well?"

"Sir!" cried Polly. "I can explain —"

"My dear girl, you can tell me very little that I have not already surmised," he replied, then turned his attention on the luckless Mr. Mayhew. "Mr. Mayhew, the queue for carriages is already forming. You would be advised to get in it without delay."

"I — I came on foot," said the sullen poet.

"Very well. If you can withdraw that appendage from your mouth long enough, I suggest you take yourself home in like manner."

There was nothing young Mr. Mayhew could do but retreat with the tatters of his dignity drawn closely about him. Alone with her rescuer, Polly studied the top button of Sir Aubrey's waistcoat with great interest, suddenly shy of meeting his gaze.

"I — I am glad you came along when you did," she confessed. "I only came outside with him for a breath of fresh air. I cannot imagine how he interpreted that to mean that I wanted him to kiss me!"

"Then it is just as well that he did not."

Polly's embarrassment fled, and she looked sharply up at the baronet. "On the contrary, sir, he most certainly did! You saw!"

Sir Aubrey shook his head. "I saw no such thing."

Any gratitude Polly might have felt quickly turned to annoyance. "One would think that I would be the best judge of whether or not I was being kissed!"

"One would certainly think so, but apparently one would be overly optimistic in making such an assumption. That, Miss Crump, was no kiss. This is."

Before she realized what he was about, he caught her up in his arms and kissed her with a thoroughness that left her knees weak. Although she was overpowered, she knew she should at least try to resist. To this end her hands moved to his chest, but once there, instead of pushing him away, they showed an alarming tendency to clutch the lapels of his coat.

"There," said Sir Aubrey somewhat breathlessly when he at last released her. "Quite a difference, is there not?"

"Oh, insufferable!" cried Polly, scrubbing at her bruised lips with the back of her gloved hand. "You are no better than he is!"

"I beg to differ, Miss Crump. I succeeded where he failed," pointed out Sir Aubrey, unrepentant.

"You are both despicable!" declared Polly, outraged. "In fact, I cannot see that there is a ha'porth of difference between you!"

"I am chastened, indeed," said Sir Aubrey, bowing deeply from the waist. "If you will excuse me, I shall endeavor to console myself."

So saying, he re-entered the house in

Mr. Mayhew's wake, leaving Polly alone and shaken. He was monstrous, and she hated him! But she had lied. She had said there was no difference between them, but that was not true. Mr. Mayhew's advances, unwelcome though they may have been, had come with a proposal of marriage, but Sir Aubrey had spoken no word on the subject. And who could blame him? There could be no question of matrimony between a baronet and a shopgirl. Confiding in him had been a foolish, and possibly fatal, mistake, for now that he knew she was not of his class, he believed he might do as he pleased with her. How could she have been stupid enough to let a small show of kindness and a pair of sea-gray eyes cloud her judgment so completely? Perhaps Mrs. Jennings was right when she said Polly was born in sin, for now it appeared she was, at heart, her mother's daughter. If her only choices were an honorable attachment with someone like Mr. Mayhew or an indecent connection with Sir Aubrey Tabor, Polly was not at all certain she possessed the moral strength to take the higher course.

Once inside Lady Belmont's crowded salon, Sir Aubrey sought out a relatively private corner where he could brood undisturbed. When he had first intervened in her obviously unwelcome *tête-à-tête* with Mr. Mayhew, his motives had been purely humanitarian; indeed, he hoped that any gentleman worthy of the name would have done the same for a lady in distress. And yet there was that feeling, engendered that afternoon on the shore, that Miss Crump's welfare was his responsibility and his alone. His kiss had been purely in the interest of asserting his prior claim — or it had been, at first. But no sooner had he felt her deliciously rounded body in his arms and tasted her soft, sweet lips beneath his than he felt a curious reluctance to let her go. More disturbing still was the realization that he had wanted to kiss her ever since the morning she'd emptied the coffeepot onto his lap. He had been so shaken by the discovery that he had instantly retreated into the rôle of bored dandy, but inside he felt as gauche and inept as — as — His lips twisted in a wry grimace. He felt as gauche and inept as a lovestruck Ethan Brundy, newly arrived in London and staring slack-jawed across Covent Garden Theater at the beautiful Lady Helen Radney.

But where his friend had wed and eventually won his lady, Sir Aubrey had not the freedom to marry to please himself. He was a baronet and the great-grandson of a marquess; he owed it to his name to make a suitable alliance with a woman who would add to his family's consequence. Love matches with the by-blows of unknown gentlemen, he reflected wryly, were out of the question.

Of course, there was another alternative, one favored by gentlemen who, like himself, found themselves enamoured of women whom, for whatever reason, they could not marry. He might set Polly up in a discreet house where they could live as man and wife without benefit of clergy. Such arrangements were common enough in his world; even the Prince Regent's brother, the Duke of Clarence, had lived in pseudo-domestic bliss with the famed actress Dorothea Jordan for twenty years, producing no less than ten little FitzClarences, and no one among the *beau monde* even lifted an eyebrow.

He rejected the idea almost at once. While he would be willing to take her on any terms, she would be the one to bear Society's censure. Polly, who might have been the Countess of Camfield, would no longer be received in polite society, and his mother and Lady Helen would be obliged to turn a blind eye to her if they ever encountered her in public. And while he would not hesitate to acknowledge and provide for any children she might bear him — not for his child the sort of uncertainty that Polly had endured! — any son of hers would be barred by law from inheriting his title. No, it was not to be thought of. He might have been tempted to pursue such a course while he still believed Miss Crump to be a scheming adventuress, but after having heard Polly's history from her own lips, only a blackguard would make her the same indecent offer proposed by her erstwhile employer — the prospect of which had been enough to drive her to spin a web of lies in order to escape with her virtue intact.

He grimaced. What singularly ugly thoughts to be entertaining about the woman he loved! And yet, what choice did he have?

Lost in thought, Sir Aubrey was not aware that he was watching the door until it opened and Polly (having lingered on the balcony long enough to recover her poise) re-entered the house. She was claimed almost at once by the stammering young Viscount Sutcliffe, who spent the rest of the evening following her about like a Tantony pig. Sir Aubrey resisted the urge to go to her; he felt singularly unprepared for another *tête-à-tête* just yet, and his cousin, being content to gaze at his goddess, was unlikely to discommode her with unwanted attentions.

The marquess of Inglewood, however, frowning as he watched his heir's courtship from the opposite side of the room, was not so sanguine. Slowly, so as not to attract undue notice, he made his way to Sir Aubrey's corner and trapped his distracted relation.

"I say, Aubrey, what do you know about the Crump chit?"

"What do you wish to know about her?" countered Sir Aubrey.

"How to get rid of her, for one thing!"

Sir Aubrey's lips twitched. "You and Ethan Brundy would seem to have a great deal in common. Are you sure you won't let me introduce you to him?"

The Marquess of Inglewood saw no humor in being likened to a weaver. "Don't change the subject, you impudent puppy! Dash it, Aubrey, my son has been making sheep's eyes at the girl ever since you introduced them — for which, incidentally, I don't thank you, sir!"

"I beg your pardon, sir. Believe me when I say that if there were any way to undo an introduction, I would be happy to oblige. I trust you have not been so foolhardy as to suggest to Sutcliffe that you find his choice inappropriate?"

"I did a great deal more than suggest it!"

"A pity. You could not have found a better way of attaching him to her."

"You'll not pin the blame on me when you were the one who first made her known to him!" the marquess informed him roundly. "You will oblige me by keeping the girl away from my son!"

"Not to appear unsympathetic, sir, but if you believe Miss Crump has designs on Sutcliffe, hadn't you best address them to Mr. Brundy? As her host, he is in a far better position to dictate her movements."

The marquess dismissed this suggestion with a snort of derision. "Bah! Having married above himself, your Mr. Brundy could hardly be expected to understand, much less sympathize with, my position. I'll have your word, Aubrey, that you'll see to it the girl doesn't entrap my son!"

Sir Aubrey withdrew an enamelled snuffbox from his pocket, flicked it open, and raised a pinch to his nostril, all the while steadily regarding the marquess

185

through unwavering gray eyes. "Very well, then, you have my word," he said at last. "Sutcliffe will not marry her."

It was a silent and awkward party of three which made its way back to the Marine Parade. Polly, seated beside Lady Tabor on the forward-facing seat of the carriage, stared fixedly out the window in order to avoid looking at Sir Aubrey, who sat opposite on the rear-facing seat and who was by all appearances intent on a study of his evening slippers. Lady Tabor, noting the reticence of her companions and drawing her own conclusions, was moved to remonstrate with them, declaring the sight of them enough to give her a fit of the dismals.

"If anything will bring on the dismals, Mama, it is a rout," replied Sir Aubrey. "I have always found these affairs a deadly bore."

"And what of you, Miss Crump?" demanded Lady Tabor. "Did you find the evening a bore, as well?"

"No," Polly confessed shyly, and with perfect truth, "although I will own I had hoped to see the Prince. What a pity that he did not attend after all!"

"Between you and me and the lamppost, he's not much to look at," confided her ladyship. "The King's sons were all remarkably good-looking men in their heyday, but they've run sadly to fat with age."

Since neither Sir Aubrey nor Miss Crump had anything to say on the subject of the royal family, Lady Tabor was free to expound at will, and in this manner they returned to the house in Marine Parade. Once inside, Polly headed straightway for her room, while Sir Aubrey charted a direct course for the bottle of brandy he knew he would find in Mr. Brundy's study. The bottle and a pair of glasses rested on a small table beside the bookcase, exactly where he had expected them to be. More surprising was the presence of Mr. Brundy, seated behind the desk penning a response to a letter which had been forwarded to him from London.

"You still here, Ethan?" asked Sir Aubrey, decanting the golden liquid into one of the glasses. "I thought you would have long since retired. I trust Lady Helen is recovered?"

Mr. Brundy nodded. "She says she is. I put 'er to bed, nonetheless," he added with a touch of wistfulness. It was not how he would have chosen to spend a rare evening alone with his wife. He watched in mild curiosity as Sir Aubrey tossed off the contents of the glass in a single gulp and reached once more for the bottle. "Aubrey, what's 'appened?"

"I owe you an apology, Ethan," confessed Sir Aubrey flippantly. "I seem to have botched the job rather badly."

Mr. Brundy leaned back in his chair and folded his arms across his chest. " 'ave you, now? In what way?"

"I've allowed myself to become attached to your Miss Crump."

Far from being shocked, Mr. Brundy merely nodded. "I've 'ad me suspicions things were 'eading in that direction."

"Well, you jolly well could have informed me!" muttered Sir Aubrey.

"What are Miss Crump's feelings, or do you know?"

Sir Aubrey pondered the question, a thoughtful frown creasing his aristocratic brow. To be sure, he had given her little enough reason to love him; from the very first, he had all but accused her outright of being a liar and a fraud. And he had been right on both counts, although her motives were not the mercenary ones he had supposed. Yet she had confided in him of her own free will, and although she had vociferously objected to his kiss after the fact, he had not forgotten the hands that

188

crushed his lapels, pulling him closer.

"I have reason to believe my cause is not hopeless," he said at last.

"So what are your intentions?"

"Intentions?" echoed Sir Aubrey.

"We've an old custom in Lancashire," Mr. Brundy explained patiently. "When we fall in love with a lady, we marry 'er."

Sir Aubrey raised a cynical eyebrow. "My dear Ethan," he drawled, "I might as well plunge a dagger into my mother's bosom!"

Leaning forward, Mr. Brundy propped his elbow on his desk and rested his chin in the cleft of his thumb and forefinger. "You'd best drop that Society act of yours, Aubrey," he advised. "It doesn't fool me. Miss Crump may not be me sister, but she is a guest in me 'ouse, and as long as I'm responsible for 'er, any advances you choose to make 'ad better be with marriage in mind."

"I say, Ethan, is this the face you show your workers? If so, I sincerely pity them!" complained Sir Aubrey, feeling ridiculously like a recalcitrant schoolboy called on the carpet by an exacting schoolmaster, when in fact he was the elder of the two men by more than a year. Reminding himself of that fact, he met his friend's gaze squarely. "To be perfectly honest, I haven't a clue as to my intentions. Marriage, I'm afraid, is out of the question."

"Why? Are you rolled up, Aubrey? Do you 'ave to marry money?"

Sir Aubrey winced at the question. "You're nothing if not blunt, are you? But no, I'm perfectly capable of supporting a wife."

"Then I don't see the problem."

"The 'problem' is that I don't know anything about her antecedents." He recited a highly edited version of the conversation they'd had that afternoon on the beach.

" 'old on a minute," Mr. Brundy interrupted this fascinating narrative. "Did she tell you why she decided to dub 'erself me sister?"

"Oh, I almost forgot the best part," said Sir Aubrey, his grim expression momentarily dispelled by a smile. "It seems that you, Ethan, are a depraved seducer of innocents, wielding your vast fortune as a weapon against the defenseless."

"*What?*"

"You will be glad to know, however, that your character is not utterly beyond redemption. Miss Crump was convinced that you would draw the line at incest."

"Was she, now? I must remember to thank 'er!"

"No, Ethan, I beg you will not mention it to her. After all, her ludicrous reading of your character was colored by her recent experiences with her employer." He paused, frowning at the golden liquid in his glass. "Is it any wonder that I wish to rescue her from such a life?"

Mr. Brundy, understanding the question to be rhetorical, did not vouchsafe a reply.

"I suppose if her father is well-born enough, such a marriage would not be despised, but what if he isn't? I wasn't exaggerating by much when I said it would kill my mother to see me make a misalliance. And who could blame her? I'm a Tabor, dash it all, related to the Inglewoods on the distaff side! I owe something to my heritage. I would't expect you to understand, not coming from the same background, but I have to think of my heir, and *his* heir."

Mr. Brundy, unimpressed, shook his head in disbelief. "I'll never understand the Quality. You'll marry women you don't like, all so you can 'ave children 'oo are twice as 'igh in the instep as *you* are!"

"I must say, those are fine words, coming from a man who married the daughter of a duke!" retorted Sir Aubrey.

"No, but I'd already decided to marry

'elen even before I knew 'oo she was. If you'll remember, I didn't know 'er father was a dook until you told me."

Sir Aubrey gave a bitter, humorless laugh. "I seem to be an expert at arranging your love affairs, don't I? Was it only a month ago that I was telling you how to achieve your own ends and still look like a hero?" He embarked on his third glass of brandy, but stayed the glass halfway to his lips. A light slowly dawned in his gray eyes, and he put the brandy down untasted. "Ethan," he said with great deliberation, "I think it is necessary that I leave you for awhile."

"Is there any chance," Mr. Brundy asked hopefully, "that you'll be taking your mum with you?"

## 12

You men have such restless curiosity!
JANE AUSTEN, *Northanger Abbey*

After extracting a promise from Mr. Brundy not to confront Polly with her misdeeds, Sir Aubrey departed Brighton the next morning. Travelling alone in his high-perch phaeton drawn by two showy chestnuts, he accomplished the fifty-mile journey to London in rather less than the usual five hours, and within half an hour of his arrival in Town presented himself at Minchin's Book Emporium. He entered that establishment just as another customer was leaving, and as a result narrowly avoided a collision. Immediately he remembered a similar incident in this very doorway, when a petite young woman in a frumpy bonnet and a dowdy stuff gown had barrelled into him on her way out. She had looked up at him for only a fraction of a second, but as if it had happened only moments earlier, he suddenly recalled with startling clarity tear-filled blue eyes set in a heart-shaped face framed by red-gold curls. Good God! It had been Polly!

He strode briskly up to the counter, more impatient than ever to settle his business with Mr. Minchin.

"Good afternoon, sir. How may I be of service to you?" asked an apple-cheeked shopgirl, bobbing a curtsy.

A crisp white apron covered her dark stuff gown, and a frilled mob cap performed a similar service for her dark curls. Sir Aubrey thought of his Polly similarly attired, and resolved from this day forward to treat shopgirls with more kindness than had previously been his wont.

"The bestowal of such a smile is surely the greatest service any man might ask for," he replied, and had the satisfaction of seeing the girl fairly beam with pleasure. "Is Mr. Minchin in? I should like to have a word with him."

"I'll inquire at once, Mr. — ?"

"Sir Aubrey Tabor."

"Yes, sir." After bobbing another curtsy, the blushing shopgirl hurried across the room to tap on a door at the rear. It opened a crack, and a feverishly whispered conversation ensued, the only part of which Sir Aubrey could distinguish was his own name. A moment later, the door closed again and the shopgirl returned, self-consciously smoothing the skirt of her starched apron.

"Mr. Minchin will be happy to see you, sir," she said somewhat breathlessly. "If you will follow me, please."

"To the ends of the earth," declared Sir Aubrey, making the girl giggle.

She tapped on the door once more, and this time it was thrown open wide to reveal a tiny room cluttered with books and papers. The only pristine surface in the chamber belonged to a wooden straight chair, a circumstance which led Sir Aubrey to believe that the stack of books piled haphazardly onto the floor beside it had been hastily removed for the express purpose of offering him a place to sit. A wasted effort, he decided, sneering disdainfully at the pinched little man who had answered the shopgirl's knock.

"Come in, Sir Aubrey, come in!" gushed Mr. Minchin, waving his noble guest into the cramped and cluttered hole. "Do sit down! What may I do for you today?"

Ignoring the man's offer of a chair, Sir Aubrey waited until the girl had withdrawn, then closed the door and leaned languidly against it. "I am looking for information, Mr. Minchin. I understand you recently had in your employ a young woman by the name of Crump."

Mr. Minchin removed his wire-rimmed spectacles and laid them on the desk, his expression perfectly blank. "Crump? I'm not familiar with the name."

Sir Aubrey smote his brow in a gesture of self-reproach. "No, no, of course you are not! You would have known her as Miss Hampton — Miss Polly Hampton."

Mr. Minchin's rather beady eyes bulged, and he shuffled through the papers on his desk with trembling fingers. "Miss Hampton? Why, yes, as a matter of fact, I hired Miss Hampton in March, but was obliged to let her go after only four months. A pretty little thing, but intolerably lazy."

"What can you tell me about Miss Cr— Hampton's background? You say you hired her in March? Was she newly arrived in London at that time?"

"With all due respect, Sir Aubrey, I can hardly be expected to recall in minute detail the affairs of everyone who seeks employment from me!"

"No doubt you are right." Sir Aubrey withdrew a golden guinea from his pocket and weighed it idly in his hand. "Pity, that."

"Of course, I could be wrong," began Mr. Minchin eying the coin greedily, "but I seem to remember Miss Hampton mentioning a village called Littledean, in Leicestershire. It seems she was raised by the vicar there."

"How fortuitous for me that you should remember," drawled Sir Aubrey, flicking the coin to the bookseller.

"As I said, her performance here was far from satisfactory. I hope you were not looking to hire her as a maid of all work?"

"You may be easy on that head, Mr. Minchin," Sir Aubrey assured him. "I have no intention of hiring Miss Crump — Miss Hampton, if you prefer — as a maid of all work."

"Only the horizontal kind, eh?" Mr. Minchin asked knowingly, as his somewhat hunted expression yielded to a curious blend of relief and lasciviousness. There was, in his opinion, only one thing a man of Sir Aubrey's stamp might want from a girl like Polly Hampton. "Well, she'll be a dainty armful, I'll grant you that. I once considered her for that position myself, but she wouldn't have me. No doubt she was holding out for bigger game."

"You seem to be laboring under some delusion as to Miss Hampton's character," observed Sir Aubrey, studying the bookseller beneath lazily drooping eyelids.

"Allow me to enlighten you."

Every trace of indolence vanished in an instant. With his left hand, Sir Aubrey grabbed the luckless Mr. Minchin by the cravat; with his right, he delivered a punishing blow to the now-terrified bookseller's nose. Mr. Minchin crumpled to an inanimate heap on the floor, gushing blood from his abused proboscis. After giving the heap a nudge with his booted foot to assure himself that his victim yet lived, Sir Aubrey opened the office door to find a goggle-eyed shopgirl staring at him in horrified fascination.

"Mr. Minchin has decided to take a nap," Sir Aubrey informed her. "He should awaken shortly very much the wiser."

And with that prediction, he betook himself from the shop.

The following evening found Sir Aubrey in the village of Littledean, where he stopped to spend the night at a hostelry bearing the ambitious appellation of The Royal Arms. As most such establishments claiming royal patronage tended to be far more ancient than this red-brick structure, his curiosity was piqued. When the innkeeper placed a bowl of stew and a large tankard of home-brewed ale on the table before him, Sir Aubrey jerked his thumb in the direction of the window, through which the red-and-gold sign could be seen swaying in the summer breeze.

"The Royal Arms?" he remarked, inviting the innkeeper to explain.

"Aye, 'twill be twenty years ago this October that His Royal Highness the Duke of Clarence occupied this very room. Sat right there before the fire, he did," added the innkeeper, pointing to the fireplace.

"He never stayed here!" said Sir Aubrey in skeptical accents, his gaze taking in not only the fireplace, but the entire room. Although it was clean enough, there was nothing in its somewhat stark appearance to recommend it to royalty.

"Well, no, not overnight," admitted his host with some reluctance. "He was visiting Lord Littledean for the hunt, so naturally he stayed at the big house with his lordship. But after the hunt, they stopped by here, and His Royal Highness finished off two tankards of my best home-brewed. That's why we call it The Royal *Arms*," he explained, "on account of he was lifting 'em so free."

Declaring his host a veritable font of information, Sir Aubrey went on to inquire as to the direction of the church, and what time he would be most likely to find the vicar at home. Having been advised on this head, he went upstairs to his room, eager to pursue his quest upon the morrow. Accordingly, he arose early, partook of a hearty breakfast prepared by the innkeeper's buxom wife, and set out on foot toward the church. This proved to be a very ancient building crafted of gray stone in the Norman tradition, with a smaller dwelling behind which Sir Aubrey assumed (correctly, as it proved) to be the vicarage. He strode up the shrubbery-lined path and knocked on the door, and was just congratulating himself on his progress when he suffered his first setback. For the black-garbed clergyman who answered Sir Aubrey's knock appeared to be several years the baronet's junior, and far too young to have reared Polly as a daughter.

"Are — are you the vicar?" asked Sir Aubrey, startled out of his usual *savoir-faire*.

"Indeed, I am Reverend Townsend," said the young man, stroking his rather long chin and regarding his visitor curiously through mild blue eyes framed by wire-rimmed spectacles. "How may I help you, Mr. — ?"

"Sir Aubrey Tabor, of Tabor Hall,

Somerset," said the baronet quickly, offering his hand as he remembered his manners. "I'm sorry to trouble you, Reverend. I was looking for — but it appears I have been misinformed."

"Perhaps so, but if you will tell me whom you are seeking, I shall do anything in my power to assist you."

Having travelled so far, Sir Aubrey decided he had nothing to lose. "I was told the vicar of this village had taken in an, er, orphan and reared her as a daughter. As the young lady is now almost twenty years old, you are far too young to be the man."

Enlightenment dawned in the vicar's eyes. "Ah! You are thinking, no doubt, of the previous vicar, Reverend Jennings. He passed to his reward a month ago, and I have only since then acquired the living here. His widow has gone to live with her sister in Northampton."

Sir Aubrey thanked the vicar for the information, then returned to The Royal Arms to prepare for yet another day's journey. But even as he set his horses' heads toward Northampton, he wondered if he were bent on a wild-goose chase. Even if he found Mrs. Jennings, it did not necessarily follow that she would furnish the name of Polly's father, even if she knew his identity. Which, wondered Sir Aubrey, would be worse: to be unable to find him, or to discover him to be someone unworthy of the Tabor connection? Damn Lord Camfield, the old lecher! Why couldn't he have been her father, like he was supposed to?

With such melancholy thoughts to accompany him, it was little wonder that by the time Sir Aubrey reached his destination late that afternoon, his spirits were drooping considerably. Stopping at a posting-house, he surrendered his winded team to the ostler and went inside in search of refreshment and information. When the former was delivered by a rotund serving-woman swathed in a voluminous white apron, he broached the subject of the latter.

"Have you any knowledge of a Mrs. Jennings, relict of a Leicestershire vicar, who arrived about a month ago? I believe she has been living with her sister since the death of her husband."

"Aye, she be the sister of Miss Whitfield. Live in Wembley Cottage, they do."

This information was delivered in a voice which, Sir Aubrey thought, he might have heard all the way from Brighton and thus spared himself the trip. Thus, it was not surprising that it caught the attention of another serving-wench, this one younger and eager to attract the notice of the handsome and obviously well-breeched stranger in their midst. Perching her tray on one generous hip, she sidled up to Sir Aubrey's table and awaited her opening as the older woman gave him directions to Wembley Cottage.

"Just follow the main road past the church, till you come to a lane leading right. Follow it until you reach the end, and then —"

"It'll take him all day to reach Wembley Cottage that route," the younger woman chided the elder, then turned the full force of her charms on Sir Aubrey. "Now, if you was to ask me, I'd tell you to turn before you get to the church, and take the footpath through the spinney."

"The spinney? He'd get lost for sure, not knowing his way 'round here," objected the other.

"Not with a guide, he wouldn't." She leaned forward and propped her elbows on the table, the better to afford Sir Aubrey an unobstructed view of bountiful bosom. "I'd be that pleased to show you the way, if you like."

The older woman planted her hands on

her ample hips and glowered at the younger, but even without that woman's patent disapproval, Sir Aubrey would have had no difficulty in surmising that, once they reached the privacy of the spinney, his escort would have been in no hurry to reach Wembley Cottage.

"Thank you, but I, er, shouldn't dream of keeping you from your duties," he demurred.

With a little huff of frustration, his would-be guide betook herself from the table, leaving the other to beam at Sir Aubrey as she might a schoolboy who had correctly ciphered a particularly difficult sum.

"As I was saying, sir, if you want Wembley Cottage, you just follow that lane right to the end, and there it'll be, big as life."

So saying, she left Sir Aubrey to enjoy his meal. The food was plain but satisfying, and yet Sir Aubrey could not quite shake the feeling that he was the main course. The younger of the two serving-women lost no opportunity to stroll past his table, often near enough that her skirts brushed his shoulder and once, when he was foolhardy enough to look up, meeting his distracted gaze with a broad wink. At one time, he would not have been averse to whiling away an agreeable hour with a game pullet who was obviously eager to oblige him. But the lures being cast out to him only served to emphasize Polly's genteel manner, and to make him all the more impatient to prove her worthy of the position to which he hoped to raise her. Strengthened in this resolve, he at last pushed his plate away, paid his shot, and set out on foot for Wembley Cottage.

Dismissing the spinney with a shudder, he held to the main road until he passed the church, then took the lane leading off to the right. It twisted and turned, bisecting green meadows where sheep grazed, then skirting the woods — the serving-maid's spinney, no doubt — for a short distance before ending at a quaint cottage. Summer flowers bloomed riotously in the garden, but there was still a deserted air about the place. Sir Aubrey had the sinking feeling that his hopes were about to be blighted once more. Nevertheless, he rapped on the front door, and a moment later it was opened by a maid wearing the ubiquitous dark dress and white apron and cap.

"Sir Aubrey Tabor, to see Mrs. Jennings," he said, giving the girl his card.

"Oh, but Mrs. Jennings ain't at home,

sir," she answered, staring wide-eyed at her mistress's elegant visitor.

Sir Aubrey suppressed a sigh. Nothing on his journey thus far had suggested it would be easy; why should he expect otherwise now? "When do you expect her home? May I wait?"

"Oh, no, sir! She's gone away with her sister. The doctor sent Miss Whitfield — Mrs. Jennings's sister, that is, only you'd never guess they was sisters, if you were to ask me —"

"Yes, yes," Sir Aubrey cut short what showed every indication of being a very lengthy comparison of the two women. "Where did the doctor send her?"

"Just a moment." Ducking back into the house, she shut the door so swiftly that she almost caught the tip of Sir Aubrey's aristocratic nose. A moment later the door opened again, and this time the maid bore a small square of paper. "I can't read, sir, but she's having all her mail sent to this direction."

Sir Aubrey took the paper and read it. Suddenly, to the little maid's utter astonishment, he threw back his head and began to laugh.

Mrs. Jennings's mail was being sent to Number 11 Bedford Square, Brighton.

## 13

Hasty marriage seldom proveth well.
WILLIAM SHAKESPEARE,
*King Henry the Sixth*

While Sir Aubrey criss-crossed England on his quest, Polly tried valiantly to convince herself that she did not miss him at all. She reminded herself daily that any man who could kiss a girl passionately one night only to leave town the very next morning had clearly proven himself to be undeserving of her regard, and therefore unworthy of a moment's melancholy reflection. Unfortunately, these lofty sentiments had the effect of adding to her misery, rather than alleviating it.

In the light of Sir Aubrey's defection, his cousin Lord Sutcliffe's obvious admiration acted as a balm to her wounded pride. It would be a rare young lady indeed who did not enjoy being adored, and the viscount's timidity guaranteed her safety from those attentions which she had found so alarming in bolder suitors. Consequently, young Lord Sutcliffe was both surprised and gratified to find himself elevated to the position of favorite. As if afraid his exalted status was destined to be short-lived, he availed himself of every opportunity to squire her about. Every day found them strolling about the Steine or riding donkeys along the clifftops overlooking the beach; every night, dancing at the Old Ship or Castle Inn assemblies. The marquess observed his son and heir's courtship with a jaundiced eye, but refrained from remonstrating with the youth again — a circumstance which said much for the marquess's faith in Sir Aubrey's word.

One sunny afternoon in early August, Lord Sutcliffe had the pleasure of accompanying Polly to the Lanes on a shopping expedition, having successfully begged the privilege of carrying her parcels. These were not likely to prove much of a burden: Polly was immensely pleased to find a pair of gloves for only four shillings, but feared sixteen was far too dear for a painted fan, be it never so fetching. Sutcliffe was quick to offer to make her a gift of it, and after protesting prettily, Polly allowed her scruples to be overruled, and they departed the shop much in charity with one another.

Once outside, however, they came face to face with two ladies intent upon entering the same shop which had so recently enjoyed their patronage. Both ladies were of a certain age, tall and somewhat frail, and one was dressed in the unrelieved black which bespoke the recent widow. Upon seeing this person, Polly's eyes opened wide with fear and the color drained from her face. She would have averted her gaze, but the widow had already recognized her, and to administer the cut direct would have created just that sort of disturbance which Polly wanted at all costs to avoid.

"M— Mrs. Jennings," she stammered, "What — what a pleasant surprise! I had no idea you were in Brighton."

"I daresay you did not," remarked the widow, disapproval writ large upon her countenance as she surveyed Polly's fashionable jaconet muslin walking dress, beribboned leghorn bonnet, and handsome young beau. "I thought you were fixed in London."

"I thought so, too, but — but I am in Brighton as the houseguest of Lady Helen Brundy," said Polly, lifting her chin a little. "Is — is this your sister? Oh, and let me introduce my escort, Lord Sutcliffe. My lord, this is Mrs. Jennings, who was kind enough to take me in when my mother died, and her sister Miss Whitfield."

"I am sure any friend of yours must be a friend of mine, Miss Crump," Lord Sutcliffe said gallantly, making an elegant leg.

"Miss Crump?" echoed Mrs. Jennings ominously.

"But we must not keep you standing on the sidewalk," Polly protested, tugging at the sleeve of Sutcliffe's coat. "I promised Lady Helen I would return in time for tea. Do call, Mrs. Jennings."

"Be sure I shall," the widow promised, and Polly could not fail to read the threat concealed within those four words. "I should like to meet this Lady Helen of yours. I'm sure we would find much to discuss."

Polly stammered an all but incoherent farewell and dragged the hapless viscount away with a most unseemly haste, her heart pounding as if it might at any moment burst. Mrs. Jennings in Brighton! Who would have supposed that her misguided search for her father would end in such disaster? Cruel experience had long since taught her that while the vicar's widow might mouth pious platitudes, there was no real Christian charity in her. No, Mrs. Jennings would not hesitate to reveal her erstwhile ward's perfidy to Lady

Helen, nor all Brighton, for that matter. Polly was a ruined creature, and all her faculties must now be devoted to finding a way to disappear before her shame became the talk of Brighton.

So all-consuming was her inner turmoil that she could not even carry on a nominal conversation with her escort. Fortunately, Lord Sutcliffe was so preoccupied with his own thoughts that he hardly noticed his fair companion's distress. When Miss Crump had first indicated a preference for his company, he had hardly dared to hope, but surely there could be no mistaking the meaning behind the trembling hand clutching his sleeve and the pleading blue eyes gazing up at him. In short, the young viscount had all the happiness of knowing that his affections were returned, and this discovery emboldened him to put his fate to the touch. Granted, Brighton's shopping district was not the most romantic setting for a proposal of marriage, but the remarkable progress of Sutcliffe's courtship over the course of the last week had made the viscount a firm believer in striking while the iron was hot, and he resolved to declare himself before his courage flagged.

"Miss Crump, you cannot have failed to notice —" Sutcliffe abandoned this approach, as Miss Crump might indeed have failed to notice, and might take offense at this seeming disparagement of her powers of observation. "Miss Crump, although you may feel that I am too young to have formed a serious attachment —" This attempt, too, was weighed and found wanting. Nothing could be gained by giving Miss Crump ammunition with which to repel his advances, and if she had not previously considered his lack of years a hindrance, it would be foolish in the extreme to bring this deficiency to her notice. The direct approach, he decided, was always the best. "Miss Crump, will you marry me?"

In truth, Polly was so consumed by her own worries that she had taken no notice of her escort's two false starts at all, save for an awareness that every repeat of that hastily assumed name seemed to remind her anew of her sins, and of the coming retribution. His blunt question, however, penetrated her consciousness with all the force of a lightning bolt. It was as if she had been drowning in the choppy waters of the Channel and someone had tossed her a lifeline. Surely once her name was Lady Sutcliffe, it would matter little what it had been before. For what had she to fear from

Mrs. Jennings with all the dignity of the Inglewood name at her command? Who would believe the venomous outpourings of a country vicar's widow over the word of the Viscountess Sutcliffe and someday Marchioness of Inglewood?

"I should be happy to marry you," Polly said without roundaboutation.

Lord Sutcliffe could scarcely believe his ears. No sooner had Miss Crump accepted his suit than he recalled in vivid detail the difficulties in breaking the news of his impending nuptials to his father. The only solution he could see was a clandestine marriage, after which he would present the marquess with a *fait accompli*. He was just drawing breath to suggest this scheme to Miss Crump, after which he was prepared to apply all his powers of persuasion to soothing her maidenly aversion to such an improper course of action, when his chosen bride took the words from his mouth.

"Only you must know that I abhor long engagements. In fact," she added resolutely, "I have always thought it would be terribly romantic to elope."

"I, too, think an elopement the very thing," he declared when he had recovered from the shock. "How much time do you need to prepare?"

After some whispered debate, it was agreed that they would slip away from the Prince's reception at the Royal Pavilion that very night. Lord Sutcliffe questioned the wisdom of this scheme, being convinced that the bride might require more time to prepare for the three-day journey to Gretna Green, but Polly, recalling Mrs. Jennings's veiled threats, was adamant. In the end, the viscount was obliged to yield.

Shortly thereafter, he returned her to the Marine Parade where she, pleading the need to rest before her presentation to the Prince Regent, locked herself in her room in order to do her packing undisturbed. Her relief at escaping what had seemed inevitable ruin was dimmed somewhat by the knowledge that in running away with Lord Sutcliffe, she was using Mr. Brundy and Lady Helen very shabbily. She could not reconcile it with her conscience to take any of the lovely gowns with which Lady Helen had so generously provided her (and for which, however grudgingly, Mr. Brundy had paid), so after lovingly fingering the numerous pastel silks and satins hanging in the clothespress, she dragged out the dreary gray gowns that had been so much a part of her former life and folded them away in the battered valise, along with such other things as she deemed necessary for a three-day journey. To these she added her most cherished mementos from her stay in Brighton: the three dog-eared volumes of *The Wicked Count* which Lady Tabor had insisted upon presenting to her, having discovered that Polly had never read this thrilling work; the beaded reticule which Lady Helen had at last completed; and the brass spyglass which Sir Aubrey had given her that day on the beach. Interestingly enough, she spared scarcely a thought for the painted fan her future husband had purchased for her that very day, although she turned Sir Aubrey's peace offering over and over in her hands, recalling in minute and exquisitely painful detail every word of their conversation.

*You haven't the bloodlines for a brilliant match.* . . . Well, Sir Aubrey Tabor would soon learn his mistake! She pictured with no small satisfaction the look on his face when he returned to Brighton and made his bow to the new Lady Sutcliffe. She would smile condescendingly and give him her fingertips to kiss. . . .

This image was less satisfying, as it brought another, most uncousinly kiss forcibly to mind. Quickly, as if the polished brass burned her hand, she flung it back into the bureau drawer, only too willing for Lady Tabor to return it to her son. Then, picturing him ogling the prettiest sea-bathers through its magnifying lens, she picked it up again, buried it in the bottom of the valise, and snapped the bag shut.

Ironically, had she taken the spyglass to the window and focused it in a westerly direction, she might have seen Sir Aubrey's high-perch phaeton turn west off the Grand Parade en route to Bedford Square. For Sir Aubrey had returned to Brighton, and so intent was he upon the culmination of his quest that he did not even stop in the Marine Parade to change his travel-stained clothes, but presented himself at the door of Number 11, Bedford Square.

The house was new; in fact, completion of the thirty-six buildings which would eventually comprise the Square was not projected for another two years. Still, as the timid little maid showed him to the drawing room, Sir Aubrey's hackles rose, as if the house were haunted by some malevolent spirit.

He identified the spirit the moment Mrs. Jennings entered the room. She was draped head to foot in black, her pale, round face pinched with distaste as she surveyed her fashionable visitor.

"Sir Aubrey Tabor, is it? I don't believe we've met." *So I can't imagine what you are doing here,* was the unspoken message.

"I regret that I have never had the pleasure, Mrs. Jennings, and must beg you to forgive me for calling in this manner. I am seeking information on a young woman by the name of Miss Polly Cr— er, Hampton."

Were it possible, Mrs. Jennings's air of disapproval became even more pronounced. "So, you've an interest in Polly, have you? I daresay I know what it is!"

"Unless you are a gypsy, Mrs. Jennings, pray spare me any attempts at fortune-telling," replied Sir Aubrey at his haughty best. "I believe Miss Hampton lived with you and your husband after the death of her mother?"

"Indeed she did, at my husband's insistence. I warned him he was nurturing a viper in his bosom, but nothing could change his mind once he was convinced of his Christian duty. He was a good man, but too unmindful of his position. What must people think, but that she was his natural child?"

Sir Aubrey had, in fact, suspected precisely that, but now found himself obliged to abandon this promising theory. Any man who truly cared for his daughter would not inflict such a hostile stepmother upon her. The thought of his Polly forced to choose between the charity of this vicious woman and the lechery of Mr. Minchin was enough to make Sir Aubrey's blood boil.

"Am I to understand, then, that you disapproved of your husband's actions?" he asked silkily.

"Indeed, you are! She was born in sin, and just like her mother, her ambitions are higher than her moral standards! You might be interested to know, Sir Aubrey, that your inamorata has been parading about Brighton under an assumed name!"

"My good woman, you can tell me very little about Miss Crump — er, Hampton — that I do not already know, save perhaps the name of her father."

"Her father?" echoed Mrs. Jennings, visibly deflated by her visitor's lack of surprise at this revelation. "Truth to tell, Sir Aubrey, I don't know."

If her first effort at disconcerting her guest had been a disappointment, this simple disclosure was a resounding success. Sir Aubrey's bored expression changed to one of despair. "You *don't know?*"

"I never knew who he was. I daresay my husband may have known, but if so, he took the secret to his grave. Her mother swore her lover was Quality, but I never believed her. Depend upon it, if that one had snared herself a gentleman, she would have been trumpeting it from the rooftops!"

And so the search was over. He would never know whether or not Polly's lineage was worthy of him; in fact, the only assurance he had that the man was a gentleman had been called into question. And yet, somewhere between his departure from Brighton and his return, he had discovered that it did not really matter at all.

"Mrs. Jennings, I thank you. You have been more help than you will ever know." As further proof of this statement, he bowed deeply from the waist, raising her black-gloved hand to his lips.

"Have I?" demanded the widow, not at all certain she was pleased to have been of assistance. "What did I do?"

"You have surmised that my interest in Miss Hampton is, er, amorous in nature, but I assure you my intentions were not dishonorable. I had hoped to ascertain that Miss Crump's — that is, Miss Hampton's — parentage was sufficiently lofty, as befitted Lady Tabor of Tabor Hall."

"Well, I trust you have no more doubts on *that* head!" Mrs. Jennings replied waspishly.

"No, indeed. In fact, fifteen minutes in your company has been enough to convince me that I would marry her if her father were Tom o'Bedlam!"

## 14

It is well done, and fitting for a princess
Descended of so many royal kings.
WILLIAM SHAKESPEARE,
*Antony and Cleopatra*

By the time Sir Aubrey returned to the house
on the Marine Parade, darkness had fallen
and its inhabitants had ascended to their various
ious chambers to prepare for that evening's
entertainment. Upon inquiring of Evers as to
the nature of this engagement, Sir Aubrey
was informed that the Prince Regent was
holding a reception at the Royal Pavilion, to
which the entire party had been invited. The
invitation had included Sir Aubrey's name as
well, should he care to attend.

No, he thought impatiently, he did *not*
care to attend. Why should he choose to
swelter in Prinny's overheated, overdecorated
dollhouse when all he really wanted was a
quiet corner where he might offer himself
heart and soul to Miss Polly Crump —
rather, Hampton. He cared not at all what
her name was, so long as she would allow
him to change it to Tabor — *Lady* Tabor.

Lady Tabor! Good God! His mother!

Almost as if his thoughts had summoned her, Lady Tabor entered the room at that moment, resplendent in purple satin.

"Well, Aubrey, I was beginning to wonder if you had abandoned me to the weaver," she remarked, giving him her cheek to kiss. "I trust your business in London was concluded to your satisfaction?"

"Not yet, but I hope it will be very soon," he answered. "Sit down, Mama. I have something to tell you."

Arching one eyebrow in unconcealed curiosity, Lady Tabor sat.

"Mama, I need not enumerate for you the responsibilities of a man in my position — marriage, providing an heir to ensure the succession — in fact, thus far it has been you who have been obliged to point them out to me. I own, I have been lax in the performance of those duties because, until recently, I had not met the lady with whom performing them would not be a punishment."

"Aubrey!" gasped his mother. "Am I to understand that you intend to marry at last?"

"If she will have me," confessed Sir Aubrey. "And to be blunt, ma'am, I doubt that you will approve of my choice. Nevertheless, she *is* my choice, and I will expect you to show her every courtesy," he added with a hint of steel in his voice.

Lady Tabor's stunned expression gave way to one of wounded innocence. "I hope I would never be rude to anyone you held dear," she sniffed, conveniently forgetting the odious Mr. Brundy.

"Be that as it may —" A slight sound made him wheel round, and for the first time since the night he had kissed her on Lady Belmont's balcony, he beheld his chosen bride. She was dressed for the royal reception in a diaphanous gown of pomona green silk that made her red-gold hair shine like a newly minted penny. Sir Aubrey Tabor, noted *bon vivant*, felt his mouth go dry.

As for Polly, she had not known of Sir Aubrey's return until she had entered the drawing room and discovered him *tête-à-tête* with his mother. She had not thought to see him again until she was safely wed, and felt caught off guard. She took a step backwards, prepared to slip away unseen, but some small sound betrayed her, and he turned.

"Miss Crump."

He bowed over her hand, but his gaze

never left her face. To Polly, trying without success to interpret the intensity in his gray eyes, it seemed as if he could see right through to her soul. She thought guiltily of the packed valise that was even now hidden under the bushes in front of the house, waiting for Lord Sutcliffe to retrieve it en route to the Royal Pavilion.

"I trust you had a pleasant journey, Sir Aubrey?" she asked with a fair semblance of calm, hoping he could not see the pounding of her heart above her *décolletage*.

He relinquished her hand with an effort. "Pleasant enough, although longer than I might have wished."

It was perhaps fortunate that this awkward reunion was interrupted by the appearance of the Brundys, both in full evening regalia. As before the Bedford rout, Lady Helen was fretting over her husband's approaching brush with royalty. Mr. Brundy, however, was as unmoved by the ordeal before him as he was unsurprised by the unexpected reappearance of his houseguest.

" 'ullo, Aubrey," he said, as casually as if he had bade his friend goodbye a scant half-hour earlier. "Care to do the pretty with us at 'is 'ighness's 'ouse? We'll wait, if you like."

Sir Aubrey declined, and so Mr. Brundy escorted the ladies to the Royal Pavilion, leaving the weary traveller a quiet house in which to contemplate his future. So pleasant did he find this pastime that he was not aware of the unmarked closed carriage that drew up before the house, nor of the furtive figure that disembarked from this equipage, snatched a scarred valise from underneath a bush, leaped back into the vehicle, and drove away.

Lord Sutcliffe, clutching Polly's valise to his chest as if it were his only protection against a hostile world, leaned back against the squabs and let out a long breath. Thus far, events (though moving more rapidly than he could have wished) were turning out well enough. His first challenge had been to ensure that the marquess went on to the Royal Pavilion alone, leaving him free to fetch his bride's belongings. This had been accomplished easily enough, as the viscount's nervous state had resulted in his ruining no less than nine cravats before achieving one which was, though respectable, certainly not one of his more felicitous efforts. To the viscount's infinite relief, the marquess had long since given up on his son and departed for the Royal

225

Pavilion without him. Now the valise had been procured, and it remained only to collect his bride and set out hell-for-leather for the Border.

Alas, therein lay the problem. For in the few hours since he had parted from Miss Crump, his image of her had undergone a rapid and disturbing change. From the goddess of his idolatry, she had descended to the plane of mere humankind, and thence to a deuced managing female who not only suggested the sort of hasty marriage that all his acquaintance would denounce as shockingly bad *ton*, but had then taken it upon herself to dictate all the particulars of the elopement when any lady of sensibility would have been faint with mortification at the prospect of so improper a course of action.

Not, to be sure, that Sutcliffe wished for Miss Crump to faint; he would have quite enough on his hands just trying to elude his father's wrath long enough to accomplish the three-day journey to Gretna, without adding the inconvenience of a vaporish female. But even though his father might well disown him for this night's work, he was still an Inglewood, and the Inglewoods were men of honor. He had pledged himself to marry Miss Crump over the anvil at Gretna Green, and marry her he would. With new determination, he looked out the window as the carriage bore him ever closer to the brilliantly illuminated Royal Pavilion, although anyone observing his melancholy expression might have supposed his carriage to be a tumbril and his destination the guillotine.

To the first-time visitor, the Royal Pavilion was truly an awe-inspiring sight. The exterior was a hodge-podge of minarets and onion domes in the Oriental style; the interior a conglomeration of crimson hangings with golden tassels, painted glass panels, gilt-edged mirrors, and winged dragons cavorting in *trompe l'oeil* skies. Polly, preoccupied with her rapidly approaching nuptials, hardly noticed these wonders, but Mr. Brundy was fully alive to the spectacle before him.

"Blimey!" he uttered, eyeing with distaste a dragon snarling down at the prince's guests from the broad green leaves of a plantain tree painted on the domed ceiling.

" 'Blimey,' indeed," agreed Lady Helen, pleased to discover that her low-born husband was, in fact, a man of taste.

"Is it just me," he wondered, studying

the malevolent dragon overhead, "or does 'e look a bit like Aubrey's mama?"

"You are *not* going to make me laugh!" scolded Lady Helen, struggling mightily to hold back a smile. "If Prinny should speak to you, you must not disparage his Pavilion, for he is immensely proud of it. He oversaw the decoration himself."

"I'll try not to 'old it against 'im," promised Mr. Brundy, and was rewarded with a glare from his adoring wife.

A short time later, a buzz of excitement marked the appearance of the Prince Regent and one of his brothers, His Royal Highness the Duke of Clarence. The crowd parted before them like the waters of the Red Sea, forming a center aisle down which the royal duo might pass. With his brother bringing up the rear, the Prince made his ponderous way down the ranks, pausing to speak to the fortunate few and acknowledging the others with a genial nod. When Lady Helen sank into a deep curtsy at his approach, he took her hands in his own rather plump ones and helped her to rise.

"Ah, Lady Helen, a Radney no more!" he exclaimed with an exaggerated sigh. "On the day you were wed, every man in England mourned."

"Every man but one, your 'ighness," put in Mr. Brundy.

"Your Highness, may I present my husband, Mr. Brundy?"

"So you're the fellow who stole Lady Helen from under the noses of half the *ton*, eh?" asked the Prince, favoring Mr. Brundy with an appraising look.

"You're too good, Your 'ighness," he said modestly, making his bow. "Most people would say as 'ow I bought 'er."

As that was precisely the rumor that had reached the Prince's ears, he was somewhat taken aback by this statement. Then, as shock gave way to mirth, he laughed aloud, leading several guests to wonder what Lady Helen's weaver had said that Prinny found so amusing.

"By Jove, I like a man who's not afraid to call a spade a spade!" exclaimed the Prince. "He'll do, Lady Helen, stap me if he won't! Tell me, Mr. Brundy, what do you think of my Pavilion?"

Mr. Brundy was not afraid to call a spade a spade, but nor was he a fool. "I've never seen anything to equal it, your 'ighness," he said with perfect truth.

"Have you seen the Saloon yet?"

For an answer, Mr. Brundy was obliged to consult his wife, who shook her head indicating the negative. "It 'as so many rooms, I can't keep them all straight," he explained.

As the Prince Regent liked his residences on the grand scale, this response could not fail to please. "The Saloon is all done in crimson and gilt, and the chintz hangings were imported from China," he boasted, unmindful that this last piece of information would hardly be welcome news to the owner of an English textile mill. "You must see it before you leave. And who pray, is this young lady?"

He turned toward a wide-eyed Polly, who had been casting furtive glances at the wide doors through which she was shortly to make her escape.

"This is our guest, Miss Crump," said Lady Helen, gently nudging Polly forward.

"Deuced handsome girl, isn't she, Clarence?" pronounced the Prince, turning to his brother for confirmation.

"Indeed she is," agreed the Royal Duke, bowing over Polly's hand. "Damme if she don't remind me of someone."

They slowly progressed down the ranks, leaving in their wake an elated Lady Helen. Her husband's demeanor had been all she might have wished, deferential but not toadying (not, to be sure, that the Prince

Regent had ever displayed any aversion to being toad-eaten), and appreciative of the Prince's notice without the least hint of grovelling. Perfection itself, in fact. Let the *ton* snub him now, after the Prince Regent had singled him out! As soon as the royal procession was through and the rigid lines collapsed into less formal groupings, Lady Helen grabbed her husband's arm and pulled him toward the door.

"Where are we going?" he asked.

"To see the Saloon, by royal command," replied Lady Helen.

Once in the corridor, however, she steered him into the nearest available chamber and, after closing the door behind them, flung her arms about his neck and kissed him squarely on the mouth.

"What's that for?" asked Mr. Brundy, when he could breathe again.

"Only that I adore you, Ethan Brundy, and I'm sorry I ever doubted you!"

"In that case, feel free to doubt me any time you like," he replied, and returned her kiss with feeling.

They might have lingered there indefinitely had the door not eventually opened furtively to reveal another couple (this one also married, albeit not to each other) hoping to use the room for the same purpose. Ironically, it was the weaver and his wife who gave a guilty start, while the illicit lovers merely shrugged and went in search of a less populated trysting place.

"We should go back," Lady Helen said, reluctantly stepping out of the circle of her husband's arms. "There is to be a singer in the Music Room, and it would look very odd if we did not put in an appearance."

"All right, love, if you — good God!" Catching sight of one of the many gilt-framed paintings adorning the walls, Mr. Brundy stepped closer to inspect it more thoroughly. " 'oo are they, 'elen?"

Lady Helen joined him in studying the portrait. No less than thirteen children, ranging in age from infancy to young adulthood, had been committed to canvas by the late Mr. Hoppner. They were richly dressed in the fashions of the previous century, their light blue eyes good-humored, their unpowdered hair incorporating every hue from light red-gold to dark auburn.

"They are the King's children," she told her husband. "The oldest is, of course, the Prince Regent, and there is the Duke of Clarence, whom you met tonight. One would never think it to see them now, but the king's sons were all remarkably handsome before they grew so fat, don't you think?"

" 'elen, don't you see?" asked Mr. Brundy, turning to regard his wife with incredulous brown eyes. "It's Miss Crump! She's a bloomin' 'anover!"

A closer inspection of the canvas led Lady Helen to believe that her husband was right, but other than resolving to ask Lady Tabor for anything she might recollect about the youthful loves of Farmer George's sons, there was very little they could do with the information until they returned home. As calmly as possible, Lady Helen took her husband's arm and allowed him to escort her to the Music Room, where a soprano was to entertain the guests with a selection of songs in Italian. As Mr. Brundy spoke not a word of any language save his native tongue (and there were those who would question his proficiency even in that), very little time elapsed before he was heartily bored with the proceedings and wished nothing more than to return to his hired house on the Marine Parade, where he might have the pleasure of informing Sir Aubrey Tabor that he lacked the bloodlines to aspire to marriage with Miss Crump.

The soprano, La Dulcianni, was chagrined to discover that one of her audience — a young and rather attractive male one, at that — was not attending her performance at all, but rather scanning the assemblage with restless eyes. Worse, she was quite certain at one point that he had raised one white-gloved hand to conceal a yawn. But far from being offended, La Dulcianni (who had begun life as Annie Lockett of Liverpool, before her formidable talent had found a patron) recognized in Mr. Brundy a kindred spirit. After a whispered exchange with her accompanist, she temporarily abandoned her Italian repertoire to sing instead a well-known English folk song.

"I care not what the old folks say, I'll take no heed or warning," she sang, with a conspiratorial smile at her fellow Lancashire countryman, "For I'll be wearing a wedding ring at Gretna in the morning."

The thunderous applause which greeted the conclusion of this ditty suggested that Mr. Brundy was not the only one who appreciated her abrupt change of program. Alas, though she had endeared herself to her audience, she had lost the attention of her primary audience. For as she rendered the final bars, a footman delivered a sealed missive to Lady Helen. After reading this epistle, she grew quite pale, so much so that Mr. Brundy, who had not forgotten his wife's recent fainting spell, became seriously alarmed.

" 'elen, love, are you all right?" he murmured under cover of the music.

"It's Polly," she whispered, clutching his sleeve. "Ethan, she's eloped!"

## 15

Mad in pursuit, and in possession so.
WILLIAM SHAKESPEARE, *Sonnet 129*

"Eloped?" Mr. Brundy snatched the note from his wife's nerveless fingers and scanned the single folded sheet.

*Dear Lady Helen,* read this missive, *by the time you read this, I shall be on my way to the Border with Lord Sutcliffe. I blush with shame when I consider that your generosity is to be rewarded so shabbily. Pray believe that only the direst of circumstances could have induced me to follow so contemptible a course of action. I only hope that, as Lady Sutcliffe, I will be in a position to repay at least a few of your many kindnesses. Give my warmest regards to your husband and Lady Tabor.* It was signed only "Polly," with no surname.

Mr. Brundy folded the note and stuffed it into the breast pocket of his coat. "Come on, 'elen, let's get out of 'ere," he said, grabbing his wife's hand.

Anxious for Polly's sake to squelch any hint of scandal, Lady Helen submitted without protest as her husband all but dragged her from the Music Room. In the corridor, however, her tongue was loosed.

"Oh, this is all my fault! If we hadn't been — that is, if I had been chaperoning her as I ought, she never would have been able to slip away!"

"Don't count on it, love. She's a resourceful young lady, our Miss Crump — as I've reason to know."

"Ethan, what are we going to do?"

"Go 'ome and fetch Aubrey."

"But what about Lady Tabor?"

"You can 'ave a message delivered to 'er while I send for the carriage."

This suggestion found immediate favor, and Lady Helen gave the necessary instructions to a footman while her husband ordered the carriage brought round. No sooner had Mr. Brundy handed her into this equipage than he was accosted by an indignant Lady Tabor.

"Well, Mr. Brundy, I hope you are satisfied," she grumbled. "As if it weren't enough, your monopolizing the Regent in that encroaching fashion —"

She got no further before she was unceremoniously bundled into the carriage. Barking orders to the coachman, Mr. Brundy climbed aboard right behind Lady Tabor, and the carriage leaped into motion.

"Mr. Brundy!" cried Lady Tabor, grasping the leather strap to avoid being bounced all over the seat. "What, pray, is the meaning of this?"

"Miss Crump is gone," he said curtly. "I promise you'll 'ear it all, but not now."

The short drive to the house on the Marine Parade was accomplished in record time, and Mr. Brundy did not even wait for the carriage to come to a complete stop before wrenching the door open and leaping out. Leaving the coachman to assist the ladies, he hurried into the house, bellowing at the top of his voice for Sir Aubrey.

That gentleman, having washed and changed out of his travel-stained clothes, was feeling much refreshed and so impatient to declare himself to his Polly that he had begun to regret his decision not to follow her to the Royal Pavilion. He had spent the better part of the evening in Mr. Brundy's study, preparing his speech and fortifying himself for its delivery with his host's best brandy. Upon hearing the commotion which heralded the party's return, he abandoned the study in order to seek a *tête-à-tête* with his chosen bride.

"Well, Ethan, that was prompt," he remarked as a breathless Mr. Brundy burst into the room. "Did you prevail upon Lady Helen to suffer another fainting spell? I thank you!"

"You'd best 'old your thanks, Aubrey," advised Mr. Brundy. "Polly's gone. She's 'eaded for the Border with Sutcliffe."

Sir Aubrey's good-humored smile faded, leaving his handsome countenance oddly green about the gills. "No!"

Mr. Brundy produced the note from his coat pocket. " 'ere, read it yourself."

Sir Aubrey hastily scanned the missive. In spite of the urgency of the moment, he took note of the fact that, although Polly gave her regards to his mother and Mr. Brundy, there was no mention of his own name. Alas, he had not the leisure to consider the implications of this curious omission.

"How long?"

Mr. Brundy did not have to ask what he meant. "The note was delivered to 'elen at midnight."

Sir Aubrey's lip curled in sardonic amusement at this display of melodrama on the part of his beloved. "By which time Polly was already long gone, I'll wager. I'm going to bring her back, Ethan. Are you with me?"

"Aye, if you wish, but you'll travel faster

alone," Mr. Brundy pointed out.

"No, we can travel through the night if need be, taking turns driving," said Sir Aubrey, who had already reached the door and was barking orders to the coachman to have his phaeton put to at once.

While these instructions were being carried out, both men hurried up the stairs to their respective chambers. When they descended a few minutes later, Mr. Brundy had exchanged his formal attire for clothing more suitable for travelling. Sir Aubrey had donned a caped driving coat, and carried under his arm a case containing a set of duelling pistols. As the phaeton was by this time waiting before the door, Sir Aubrey was impatient to leave at once. Mr. Brundy followed him as far as the front door, then lingered to kiss his wife goodbye — a process which threatened to prove so protracted that Sir Aubrey was at last compelled to seize his friend by the collar and wrest him bodily from his bride's arms.

"Mama," Sir Aubrey tossed over his shoulder to where an uncharacteristically speechless Lady Tabor had collapsed onto the sofa, having by this time been brought up to date by Lady Helen, "if I have not returned with Miss Crump by morning, I want you to have the marquess escort you to Inglewood. I shall join you there shortly, bringing with me either my wife — or Sutcliffe's widow!"

With every mile that passed beneath his horses' hooves, Lord Sutcliffe grew more and more convinced that he had made a dreadful mistake. To be sure, Miss Crump was beautiful and he was desperately in love with her, but his ardor cooled considerably every time he thought of his father. Putting his head out the window of the closed carriage, he could almost see the marquess hot on his trail, fire issuing from his nostrils and promises of vengeance pouring from his lips.

"Do get your head back inside and close the window!" beseeched his love rather more tartly than became a runaway bride.

"I was just looking to see if we were being pursued," said Lord Sutcliffe defensively.

"Well, if we are, all the more reason for keeping your head in the carriage!" retorted Polly with inarguable logic. "What time is it?"

Lord Sutcliffe withdrew his pocket watch and held it to the window, allowing the light from the full moon to illuminate its face. "Twenty minutes past two o'clock."

"Lady Helen will have long since had my note, then," she remarked, more to herself than to her affianced husband.

"Note?" echoed the viscount in alarm. "You left a *note?*"

"I instructed a footman to deliver the note at twelve o'clock — two hours after we left. Depend upon it, if anyone is following us, they are far behind. After all, I could hardly disappear into the night without a by-your-leave," she pointed out, trying not to remember that she had once promised Sir Aubrey to do precisely that — whereupon he had threatened to come after her and thrash her soundly, as she recalled. Instead, it had been he who had disappeared without a word of farewell.

Unlike Sutcliffe, Polly had no fear of being pursued; who, she reasoned, would want her? She was neither fish nor fowl, neither genteel enough (as Sir Aubrey had been kind enough to point out) to make a Society marriage, nor quite common enough, thanks to her brief taste of fashionable life, to return to her previous existence. For even if she were fortunate enough to procure another position, how could she face her noble clients in such a servile capacity after rubbing shoulders with them at the Royal Pavilion? There remained in between only the shadowy world of the *demi-monde,* and when she had discovered Mrs. Jennings in Brighton, it had appeared that ruin of one kind or another was to be her inevitable fate. Only Lord Sutcliffe's providential proposal of marriage had offered her an escape route, and for that, she reminded herself firmly, she owed him her lifelong gratitude, even if she could not give him her love. That, it seemed, was no longer hers to give, for it had long since belonged to the only bachelor in Brighton who did not want it.

When Lady Helen awoke the next morning to find herself alone in the bed, she could only assume that Sir Aubrey had not yet run his quarry to earth. Distressing as the thought was, it was more comforting than the ominous possibility that he had overturned his phaeton, and that her husband was at that moment lying dead in a ditch somewhere along the Great North Road.

Remembering Sir Aubrey's parting instructions to his mother, Lady Helen resolved to assist Lady Tabor in preparing for her departure, even though she was not feeling at all well — the result, no doubt, of a troubled night spent listening for the sound of her husband's footsteps in the hall below. Slipping a frilled wrapper over her nightrail, she descended the stairs to the breakfast room, where a number of silver chafing dishes were lined up on the buffet. But Lady Helen had little appetite, and so she spurned heartier fare in favor of a cup of coffee and two slices of toast.

"Good morning, Lady Helen," said the dowager, already dressed in a blue kerseymere travelling ensemble. "I gather the travellers have not yet returned."

"I fear you are right, my lady. I only hope Sir Aubrey has not landed them in the ditch."

"You may rest easy on that head," replied Lady Tabor, filling a plate from the silver chafing dishes to fortify herself for the journey ahead. "My son may be utterly useless in every other way, but he can drive, as they say, to an inch. I suppose he means to have that girl," she concluded with a sigh.

"I can assure you, Lady Tabor, the match would not be as unequal as you might think. Mr. Brundy believes her to be a Hanover, on the wrong side of the blanket, of course, and after seeing a certain painting last night at the Pavilion, I am inclined to agree with him."

"Much as it galls me to agree with your husband, I fear I must. I wonder which one is the father? Clarence, I daresay; he's proven himself quite proficient at that sort of thing."

Lady Helen was startled into spilling her coffee. "You knew?"

"I thought she looked familiar the first time I saw her. It was not difficult to deduce the rest."

"But — why didn't you say so?"

"My dear Lady Helen, one must never comment on a likeness," replied Lady Tabor, crossing the breakfast room to place her laden plate on the table. "The results can be most embarrassing."

As the dowager took her place at the table, the aroma of buttered eggs and fried bacon assailed Lady Helen's nostrils. Her green eyes grew wide with alarm and, clapping one hand over her mouth, she leaped up from the table and ran from the room.

Lady Tabor, fearing the worst, followed quickly in her wake and found her hostess in her bedchamber, somewhat violently emptying the contents of her stomach into a white porcelain washbowl. Without further ado, she led the weak and trembling

Lady Helen to sit down at the dressing table.

"I do apologize," gasped Lady Helen when she had finished retching. "I can't imagine what came over me."

"Can you not?" asked Lady Tabor with interest as she bathed the sufferer's brow with a damp cloth. "I had my suspicions the night you fainted at Lady Belmont's rout. Tell me, Lady Helen, have you considered that you might be with child?"

It was quite obvious from Lady Helen's awed expression that she had not considered such a possibility. "Oh, my lady! Do you truly think so?"

"Of course I cannot be certain — you will want to see an *accoucheur* for that — but having borne five children of my own, I would own myself much shocked if I could not recognize that condition when I see it in another woman."

A baby, marveled Lady Helen. A boy, perhaps, with his father's brown eyes and soft black curls. She could almost see him in her mind's eye when Lady Tabor's voice shattered this picture.

"— remove to Reddington Hall for Christmas and remain there for the birth, as the duke will no doubt wish for his first grandchild to be born there —"

"No, the baby will be born at my husband's house in Lancashire," Lady Helen said decisively.

"Lady Helen!" cried the dowager, appalled. "You cannot wish your child to be born practically in the shadow of a cotton mill!"

"As the child will someday own the cotton mill, I think it highly appropriate," replied Lady Helen placidly.

It was evident that Lady Tabor had not spared a thought for the child's paternity. "Another weaver!" she said, suppressing a shudder. "Good heavens!"

While a maid saw to the packing of her belongings, Lady Tabor unburdened herself of a great deal of maternal advice which Lady Helen, having no mother to turn to for this sort of information, greedily absorbed. In fact, both ladies were equally disappointed when the marquess arrived to fetch his cousin long before she reached the bottom of her store of wisdom.

While a footman loaded her bags onto the marquess's crested carriage, Lady Tabor embraced her hostess warmly and bade her a fond farewell. "Though I am convinced that Aubrey would not go so far as to shoot young Sutcliffe, I shall write and tell you the outcome. In the meantime, do take care of yourself, my dear. Pray offer my congratulations to your husband, and give him my thanks for his hospitality, grudging though it was. I suppose you are in love with him — a pity, but I suppose it can't be helped. If I were thirty years younger, I daresay I should be more than a little in love with him myself."

Having delivered herself of this astonishing speech, Lady Tabor marched as far as the door, then turned back to fix her hostess with a gimlet stare. "And if you ever intimate to your husband that I said such a thing, I shall deny it with my dying breath!"

Darkness fell as Sir Aubrey drew his phaeton to a stop in the yard of the Rose and Crown, a bustling posting-house just outside Harrowgate. They had been on the road for two days, travelled almost two hundred and fifty miles, and although Sir Aubrey made inquiries at every stop, they had yet to apprehend the runaways. Twice they had been told that a young couple fitting their quarry's description had stopped to change horses, but when pressed, the ostlers could not say with any certainty what time this transaction had taken place. Mr. Brundy's eminently reasonable suggestion that Sir Aubrey might find his sources more forthcoming if he would restrain himself from seizing them by the throats while making his interrogations fell on deaf ears.

While the ostler harnessed a fresh team to the phaeton, Sir Aubrey and Mr. Brundy went inside in search of refreshment. They had not slept in two days, and Mr. Brundy longed for his bed, but as Sir Aubrey was more than a little crazed by any suggestion that Polly and Sutcliffe might have broken their journey for the night, he wisely held his tongue.

After requesting a repast of bread and cheese (which might be easily consumed on the road), Sir Aubrey got to the business at hand. "Do you recall having seen a young lady and gentleman, oh, about twenty years of age, stop here? The gentleman is dark, the young lady fair-haired and quite pretty?"

"Why, funny you should ask, sir," remarked the innkeeper, setting down two foaming tankards of ale. "We have such a couple upstairs at this very minute. Wanted a room right hasty. Give me two guineas, they did and no questions asked," he added, winking broadly at his guests.

Sir Aubrey did not wait to hear more.

"What room?" he demanded, on this occasion reserving his more violent questioning techniques for the hapless Sutcliffe.

"Upstairs, fourth room on the right," volunteered the innkeeper.

Knocking over his chair in his haste, Sir Aubrey quit the taproom and took the stairs two at a time. He counted off the doors until he came to the fourth, then pounded on it with his fist.

"Open up, Sutcliffe! I know you're in there!"

No one answered, but the sounds of scurrying movements betrayed the presence of more than one occupant.

"If you don't open up, I'm coming in after her!"

Still no response. Sir Aubrey put his booted foot to the door and kicked it off the hinges. A wide-eyed young lady sat upright in the middle of the bed clutching the sheet to her chin, while her devoted swain waved his fists menacingly at the intruder. Sir Aubrey had never seen either one of them before in his life.

"Oh!" he exclaimed inadequately. "I seem to have made a mistake — I beg your pardon! Do, er, carry on," he said, and closed the door as best he could.

He turned to discover that he had attracted a small crowd, the primary members of which were Mr. Brundy and the innkeeper.

"You broke my door down!" accused the latter. "You'll pay me for the damage to my property, if you don't mind!"

Sir Aubrey made no attempt to refute this charge, but obligingly dug his hands into his pockets. Alas, while these had been plump enough when he had left Brighton two days earlier, the frequent changes of cattle had put a considerable drain on his purse.

"Ethan, if you would be so good as to pay the man for his door, I'll repay you as soon as we get back."

Mr. Brundy delved into his own pockets and produced only half a dozen crown pieces and a few pence. "Sorry, Aubrey, but I 'aven't got it on me."

This answer found no favor with Sir Aubrey. "Do you mean to tell me that one of the richest men in England goes about with less than two pounds in his pockets?"

"If I'd known that you intended to drag me up and down the length of England, demolishing posting-'ouses along the way, I'd've paid a visit to me banker first," replied Mr. Brundy, his voice heavy with irony.

"No, you'd have had me committed to Bedlam, and rightfully so," acknowledged Sir Aubrey with a shaky laugh. "I suppose I shall have to leave the man my watch."

At first the innkeeper proved resistent, arguing that he ran a posting-house, not a pawnshop. But upon seeing Sir Aubrey's handsome gold timepiece, he was moved to reconsider. Surely only a man of considerable means would own such a piece, and even if they never returned to redeem it, he should be able to sell it for far more than it would cost to repair his door. Pocketing his treasure, he smiled benignly upon his guests, assured them that all was forgiven, and bowed them from the premises.

Alas, Sir Aubrey's difficulties were only beginning. The next change of horses relieved Mr. Brundy of the rest of his purse, forcing Sir Aubrey to pawn first his cravat-pin, then his fob, and lastly his signet ring in order to finance the journey. There was no longer any question of stopping for the night, as they had no way to pay for such a luxury, and so they continued to press northward with Mr. Brundy taking a turn at the reins, staving off the slumber that threatened to overtake him by whistling under his breath.

Sir Aubrey, having not been present at

the Royal Pavilion, had not been privy to La Dulcianni's performance, but the tune which Mr. Brundy whistled was well-known. Sir Aubrey identified it at once, and rounded on his friend.

"Will you stop whistling that damned song?"

As Mr. Brundy had merely chosen the last song to reach his ears, he was somewhat taken aback by this response, but upon recollecting that the popular ditty involved a Gretna marriage, he wisely conceded to his friend's reasonable, if somewhat vociferously stated, request.

They crossed the bridge over the River Sark and into Scotland as dawn broke, more than thirty-six hours after departing Brighton. From there it was less than a mile to Gretna Hall, an unremarkable edifice save for the unmarked closed carriage drawn up before the door. Sir Aubrey reined in his grays and paused only long enough to remove one of his duelling pistols from its case before disembarking and striding purposefully toward the door.

"Look 'ere, Aubrey," began Mr. Brundy, following hard on his heels, "I don't pretend to be an expert on *ton* ways, but I'm sure 'elen would say it's not all the thing for you to go shooting at your cousin."

"Stand clear, Ethan," advised Sir Aubrey. "I shouldn't want you to get hurt."

Flinging the door open, he demanded of the landlord the location of the marriage room. That worthy, who made a handsome living on clandestine marriages, opened his mouth to express his regrets that the marriage room was at that moment occupied, then saw the gun in Sir Aubrey's hand and thought better of it.

"Y-You'll f-find it upstairs, sir," he stammered.

Sir Aubrey dashed up the narrow flight of stairs and paused before a closed door behind which muffled voices could be heard. He flung it open and beheld a young couple standing before a rotund priest. The bridegroom appeared stiff and nervous, and his clothing, though well-tailored, was travel-stained. The bride, whom he held by the right hand, was dressed in a rumpled gown of dark gray stuff, her riotous red-gold curls determinedly escaping from a prim knot. Sir Aubrey's throat tightened. How had he ever set foot into that accursed bookstore without noticing her at once? Even in frumpy gray stuff, she was still the most beautiful, the most desirable woman he had ever seen — and she was marrying another man.

"Do you take this woman you hold by the right hand to be your lawful wedded wife?" asked the priest in a rather bored voice, as if he had performed the ceremony so many times that it no longer held any particular interest for him.

Sir Aubrey trained his weapon on his cousin's head. "Say 'I do,' Sutcliffe, and those will be the last words ever to pass your lips."

*16*

We that are true lovers run into
strange capers.
WILLIAM SHAKESPEARE, *As You Like It*

"Sir Aubrey!" gasped Polly, whirling about to
see the baronet framed in the doorway. His
clothing was rumpled and he needed a shave,
but the cold light in his gray eyes was every
bit as menacing as the weapon in his hand.
Polly's whole body began to tremble violently,
not from fear but from some other emotion
she dared not examine too closely. Nevertheless, she held her chin at a defiant angle, and
when she spoke, her voice never wavered.

"Is my mongrel blood so objectionable,
then, that you would spill your cousin's before allowing it to be so tainted?"

The lethal light in Sir Aubrey's eyes was
extinguished, and he blinked at Polly.
"Good God, woman, is that why you think
I am here?"

"I — I can't think of any other reason to
account for your presence," said Polly, suddenly breathless. "I should think that
nothing less saving your cousin from a di-

sastrous marriage would propel you this far north — or do you have business in Scotland as well as London?"

"Did you never think that *you* might be that business? My dear girl, I have been scouring England trying to identify your father so that I might make you an offer in form!"

"And am I to understand by this declaration that he proved worthy of you?" Polly asked.

"I'll not deny that was my original concern," Sir Aubrey acknowledged. "But by the time I returned to Brighton, I had made up my mind to marry you no matter who had sired you."

If Sir Aubrey expected his lady fair to fall into his arms, he had much mistaken his Polly.

"How very big of you, to be sure!" she retorted. "I am overcome with gratitude."

Up to this point, the viscount had been so afraid that the fatal words might escape his lips that he judged it safest to say nothing at all. Gradually, he assimilated the information that Sir Aubrey had not come at the behest of the marquess, as he had feared, but because he wished to marry Miss Crump himself. Unfortunately, any relief he might have felt at this unexpected turn of events was short-lived. It was one thing to be delivered at the eleventh hour from a marriage which one had discovered was not nearly so desirable as one had originally supposed; it was quite another, however, to have one's bride stolen at the altar by one's older and more dashing cousin.

"Now, look here, Cousin Aubrey," he said, staring bravely down the barrel of the pistol still aimed at his forehead. "Miss Crump is going to marry me!"

"If she does, Sutcliffe, I can assure you that she will be a widow before she is ever a wife," responded Sir Aubrey.

At this juncture, the parson judged it time to intervene. "Gentlemen, gentlemen," he said soothingly, "I am sure we can settle this in a calm and reasonable manner. If you will put down your weapon, sir?"

With some reluctance, Sir Aubrey laid aside his arms.

"Now, my dear," continued the parson, turning his attention to Polly, "which one of these gentlemen do you intend to marry?"

"Be careful 'ow you answer, Miss Crump," advised Mr. Brundy, entering the room behind Sir Aubrey. "If I understand

258

Scottish law a-right, declaring your intention to wed before two witnesses is just as binding as if you'd joined 'ands in St. George's, 'anover Square."

Polly wavered indecisively, studying first one suitor, then the other. Lord Sutcliffe glanced nervously about the room, his eyes wide and frightened in his ridiculously boyish face. Sir Aubrey gave her back look for look, with an intensity in his gaze that she could not begin to interpret.

"You needn't marry either of them if you don't want to," Mr. Brundy said gently.

"Whose side are you on, anyway?" demanded Sir Aubrey, incensed.

"Believe me, Aubrey, an unwilling bride can be the very devil," Mr. Brundy assured him with a reminiscent gleam in his eye.

"But it has not yet been established to my satisfaction that Miss Crump is unwilling," insisted Sir Aubrey, advancing upon his intended.

"You behold me standing before the parson with another man, and yet you believe that I should prefer to marry you?" cried Polly, outraged. "Oh! You are despicable!"

"And you are adorable," he replied, taking her in his arms. Any protest she might have uttered was smothered as his lips claimed hers. As on that earlier occasion at the Belmont rout, she raised her arms to push him away, but again they betrayed her, wrapping themselves instead around his neck.

"Now," he said when he at last released her, "look me in the eye and tell me you love my cousin."

Up came Polly's chin. "I'll have you know I am extremely fond of Lord Sutcliffe!"

" 'Extremely fond'?" Sir Aubrey echoed mockingly.

"He — he has been most kind to me at a time when I was in desperate need —"

"Tell me you love him, Polly," commanded Sir Aubrey, pinning her with a look.

Polly struggled valiantly, but her determination crumbled under his gray gaze. "I — I cannot! I am sorry, Lord Sutcliffe, and I will always be grateful to you, but I cannot marry you! But," she added quickly, turning back to Sir Aubrey, "it does not follow that I will marry you instead!"

"Why not?" he persisted.

"Can you not see? Surely the inequality of such a match —"

"I've told you it doesn't matter!"

"Of all the arrogance!" cried Polly. "So long as *you* are prepared to accept *me,* then *my* feelings are of no concern! Perhaps it doesn't matter to you, but it matters a great deal to me! I will not allow you to wed me in a fit of charity, only to fling my humble origins in my face every time you are out of temper with me!"

"Er, begging your pardon, Miss Crump," put in Mr. Brundy, clearing his throat, "but the shoe seems to be on the other foot."

Two pairs of eyes, one light blue, one sea gray, turned to stare at him.

"What do you mean, Ethan?" asked Sir Aubrey.

"There's a picture 'anging in the Royal Pavilion that bears an uncanny resemblance to Miss Crump. If I were a betting man, I'd lay you odds she's a royal by-blow."

Polly's eyes grew round with amazement. *"Royal — ?"*

Sir Aubrey slapped his hand to his forehead. "The Royal Arms! The Duke of Clarence visited Littledean twenty years ago. I was that close, and never knew it! Ethan, why didn't you tell me?"

"With all the 'ullabaloo, it slipped me mind. Besides," he added with exaggerated

261

innocence, "you said it didn't matter."

"Nor does it," replied the baronet, seizing Polly's hands and drawing her inexorably closer. "In fact, the only possible obstacle I can perceive would be the discovery that Miss Crump does not love me, and if that is the case, then I am of all men the most to be pitied. For I do love you, Polly. Very, very much."

This last was delivered with a tenderness she had not heard in his voice before, and she felt the last of her resistance crumble. She tried to extricate her hands from his grasp, only to find they were trembling too violently to obey her wishes. "And if I marry you, you'll not call me by that ridiculous name, or denigrate my dancing, or —"

"Never again!" vowed Sir Aubrey.

Polly gave him a shaky smile. "What a bouncer! You have bullied me for so long I doubt you could stop even if you tried. Still, I daresay I shall not be utterly defenseless, so long as I make sure there is always a pot of coffee at the ready, and — oh, Aubrey!" Her voice broke on a sob as she was crushed in an embrace which knocked the breath from her body.

The parson heaved a sigh, rolled his eyes heavenward, and turned his prayer book back to the first page of the marriage service.

As weddings go, it was a rather shabby affair, certainly unworthy of a Tabor of Tabor Hall and a daughter — even an illegitimate one — of a royal duke, but neither of the principals seemed to mind, or in fact even to notice. The bride requested a room in which she might exchange her gray stuff gown for something a bit more bridal, and was shown into a small bedchamber. She emerged a short time later, having dressed her hair in a more becoming style and arrayed herself in the elegant but sadly crushed green gown she had worn to the Royal Pavilion.

The marriage room, however, was empty save for the cleric and Mr. Brundy, the latter standing beside the window and gazing down into the yard below. Upon Polly's entrance, he turned to regard her with his singularly sweet smile.

"Aubrey should be back shortly. 'e's borrowed a razor and a clean cravat from Lord Sutcliffe."

"Oh," said Polly, suddenly shy at finding herself alone with the man she had once claimed was her brother. "I daresay you would be grateful for a shave, yourself."

He shook his head. "No need to delay the wedding on account of me. I've waited this long; I can wait a bit longer."

She took a deep breath. "Mr. Brundy, there are so many things for which I must beg your pardon that I hardly know where to begin. We — Aubrey and I — have not had an opportunity to discuss such things as pin-money and the like, but I promise to repay you every farthing spent on my behalf —"

Mr. Brundy shook his head. "If it's your gowns you're thinking of, consider them a wedding gift from me wife."

"But not from yourself, Mr. Brundy?"

"No, I intend to give you something different. I promise not to go next or nigh the pair of you for at least three months." Seeing her bewildered expression, he added, "Aubrey will understand."

A clean and shaven Sir Aubrey entered the room at that moment with Lord Sutcliffe in his wake, and the ceremony commenced.

"Join right hands, please," instructed the parson. "Sir, do you have a ring?"

Sir Aubrey reached for his signet ring, but found only bare knuckle. "I had one, Reverend, but I, er, pawned it at Carlisle for a change of horses."

"You pawned your ring for a change of horses?" echoed Polly in amazement.

"I had no choice. All my money was gone, and it was the only thing of value I had left. I hadn't pursued you for three days only to let a lack of funds stop me less than twenty miles from my destination!"

"I think," said Polly with great deliberation, "that that is quite the loveliest thing anyone has ever done for me!"

"I have every intention of spoiling you shamelessly, my love, but I'm afraid it doesn't help much at the moment," Sir Aubrey confessed.

" 'ere's your ring, Aubrey," said Mr. Brundy, reluctantly slipping the gold band from his own finger. "Take good care of it."

"I say, Ethan, that's deuced handsome of you!" Sir Aubrey was moved to exclaim.

Mr. Brundy merely shrugged. " 'Tis the least I can do for me sister."

The ceremony completed, Sir Aubrey and his bride set out for Inglewood in Lord Sutcliffe's hired chaise. Finding herself alone with her bridegroom for the first time since the Belmont rout, Polly fell victim to an uncharacteristic shyness. Studiously avoiding his gaze, she kept her eyes demurely lowered, toying with the borrowed ring on the third finger of her left hand.

"It — it was very good of Mr. Brundy to lend his ring for the ceremony," she said at last, when the silence grew awkward.

"Ethan is the best of men, as I seem to recall telling you at one point," he reminded her. "You might have saved us all a great deal of trouble if you had believed me."

"I am sorry to have been so troublesome," she said, studying the arrangement of his borrowed cravat with great interest. "Reverend Jennings always deplored my tendency to act without thinking, but now that we are wed, I shall do my best to be a — a conformable wife."

"Good God!" uttered Sir Aubrey, appalled. "I forbid you to try! If you must know, I find your queer starts oddly enchanting, and I am sure that someday, after we have been married a very long time, I will understand perfectly why, having discovered that you loved me, you elected to elope with my cousin."

"I would never have done such a thing had my case not been desperate, I assure you!"

"You trusted me that day on the beach,

Polly. Did I prove so unworthy a confidante?"

Polly hung her head. "Not at the time. But when you — you kissed me at the Belmont rout only to disappear the very next morning, I thought that I had made a dreadful mistake, that knowing me to be nothing but an insignificant shopgirl, you felt you might treat me as you wished."

Another man might have been offended by so unflattering a portrayal, but Sir Aubrey understood that her mistrust was based on bitter experience. "And so I was not there when you needed me. I shall not soon forgive myself for that, but I cannot be entirely sorry for going to London. I had, er, unfinished business with your Mr. Minchin."

Polly paled at this revelation. "You met Mr. Minchin? Did you tell him about me? What did he say?"

"Yes, I met Mr. Minchin; yes, I told him I was searching for information concerning you; and no, he didn't say anything to the purpose."

"*Nothing?* Well, I think that rather poor-spirited of him!"

"Er, as I recall, he was lying insensible on the floor at the time," confessed Sir Aubrey.

"Aubrey! You *struck* him?" Polly gazed at her husband with a look of such adoration that he felt compelled to pull her into his arms and kiss her thoroughly.

"And while St. George was out slaying dragons for you," he chided upon the completion of this pleasant exercise, "you were plotting to elope with Sutcliffe!"

"I know it was very wrong of me, but at the time I felt I had no choice," Polly insisted. "You see, Lord Sutcliffe had accompanied me on a shopping expedition, and we encountered Mrs. Jennings — I lived in her house after my mother died, and I had no idea she was in Brighton. And when she heard Lord Sutcliffe address me as Miss Crump, she knew it was not my real name, and I was quite certain she would expose me, because that is just the sort of person she is! Believe me, Lord Sutcliffe's proposal seemed a godsend!"

"As it turns out, I have met your Mrs. Jennings, and a more poisonous female it has never been my misfortune to encounter," replied Sir Aubrey with feeling. "Making her acquaintance served to explain a great many of your actions of late, my love, but now you may rest easy. Lady Tabor need have no fear of Mrs. Jennings."

"Aubrey! Has she some hold over your *mother?*"

"My dearest goose, *you* are Lady Tabor!" pointed out Sir Aubrey, torn between exasperation and amusement.

"Oh, dear!" cried Polly in some consternation. "I suppose I am!"

"And let me tell you, this is the last name change I intend to tolerate!"

"But Aubrey, what will your mother say?"

"As she should be waiting for us at Inglewood, we shall very soon find out," he replied complacently as the carriage turned and passed through intricately wrought iron gates. A long, raked gravel drive passed through woods that suddenly fell away, revealing a broad ornamental lake across which glided a pair of graceful white swans. A massive edifice of rose-colored brick was reflected on the mirror-like surface of the water.

"Oh, how magnificent!" exclaimed Polly, leaning forward to stare out the window. "What is it?"

"It is the Marquess of Inglewood's principal seat, and my mother's childhood home."

"Oh, dear!" uttered Polly in faltering tones.

Seeing his bride's awe-stricken expression give way to one of sheer terror, he was driven by some demon of mischief to add, "Had you married Lord Sutcliffe, you would have been mistress of it someday. As it is, I fear you are doomed to disappointment, for Tabor Hall is not nearly so imposing."

"And your mother is there now?"

Sir Aubrey nodded. "Along with Lord Inglewood."

"She will not be pleased to discover you are married."

"Nonsense! She has been after me to marry for years. She should be delighted that I have finally followed her excellent advice."

"You may be sure she expected you to marry someone like Lady Helen!"

"Ethan might have had something to say about that," Sir Aubrey replied as the carriage rolled to a stop. In the next instant, the postilion opened the door and put down the step.

"Aubrey, I can't!" Polly whispered, panic-stricken, shrinking back against the squabs.

"Yes, you can," Sir Aubrey replied gently but firmly. He assisted his bride to alight, then drew her hand through his arm and gave her fingers a reassuring squeeze. "Remember, my love, the blood royal flows in your veins, and I will be there to support you through the ordeal."

Royal blood or no, Polly felt distinctly inferior as she and Sir Aubrey were admitted by a stately butler and informed that Lord Inglewood and Lady Tabor awaited them in the Green Saloon. As they climbed a broad curved staircase, Polly's fingers clenched convulsively on her husband's sleeve. At the top of the stairs, the sounds of voices emanating from a room halfway down the corridor gave her to understand that this was their destination, and so she was unsurprised when Sir Aubrey paused outside this chamber, disengaged her hand from his sleeve, and went forward to greet his mother.

"Good afternoon, Mama, Inglewood," he said, nodding to the marquess and then bending to kiss his mother's cheek. "I have someone I should like you to meet. Allow me to present — my wife."

He turned to the door and held out an imperious hand. Polly took a steadying breath, then advanced tentatively to place her hand in his. Smiling his approval, Sir Aubrey raised her hand to his lips.

"Well, young lady, you seem to have led

my son a pretty dance," observed the dowager.

Polly, bobbing a shy curtsy, could not agree. "Oh, no, my lady," she demurred. "Aubrey will be the first to tell you that my dancing is not pretty at all."

"Aubrey is an idiot," stated his fond parent. "Am I to understand that you love him anyway?"

"Yes," replied Polly — quite unnecessarily, in fact, for as she glanced up at her husband, her answer was readily visible in her glowing eyes. "Oh, yes!"

"Then that is all I could wish for," Lady Tabor said, and folded her daughter-in-law in a fond embrace.

"My felicitations to you both upon your marriage," said Lord Inglewood, bowing over Polly's hand. "I do trust, Aubrey, that you managed to bring it off without shooting my son?"

"Barely, sir, but yes," his nephew assured him. "When last I saw him, Sutcliffe was alive and well."

"And where, pray, is he now?" The marquess's tone suggested that Lord Sutcliffe would not enjoy the reunion.

"He should be arriving shortly in my phaeton. I allowed him to drive it in exchange for his bride, his razor, and a clean cravat. Now you know what a high value I place on you, my love," he added as an aside to Polly. "I don't surrender the ribbons of my phaeton to just anyone."

A commotion in the hall below heralded the arrival of Lord Sutcliffe, and a few moments later the viscount entered the room, accompanied by Mr. Brundy.

"Well, Sutcliffe, I trust you were able to keep it out of the ditch?" asked Sir Aubrey.

"Oh, Lord yes!" answered the viscount cheerfully. "You taught me to drive, didn't you? I say, Papa, Cousin Aubrey's high-perch phaeton is something like! Could I have — ?" Lord Sutcliffe saw his father regarding him with a stony countenace and, too late, remembered his disgrace. "Er, that is, I —"

"Sutcliffe," the marquess began, choosing each word with care, "although every young man falls into scrapes from time to time, I have always considered myself most fortunate in my heir — until now."

"Oh, pray do not be too hard on Lord Sutcliffe," beseeched Polly. "The idea to elope was mine, not his. Lord Sutcliffe acted entirely through chivalry, and his behavior was always that of a gentleman. If anyone is deserving of censure, my lord, it

is I. I know I have been very foolish —
Aubrey says so, anyway," she added,
darting a warm glance at her husband.

At this juncture Lady Tabor, noticing
that her daughter-in-law was looking worn
to the bone, insisted that she take a seat.
"Now, do tell us, Polly, *why*, if you loved
my son, did you ask Sutcliffe to elope with
you?"

Thus called upon, Polly was obliged to
repeat the whole tale, from the time she
first read *The Lost Heir* and conceived what
she now saw as a ridiculously naïve plan to
find her father. Her narrative encompassed
her ill-fated stint in Mr. Minchin's shop
and subsequent termination, and the
chance remark which led her to Mr.
Brundy. His entrance into the plot reminded her that she still wore his ring, and
she digressed momentarily to restore it to
its rightful owner with her heartfelt thanks.
Having done this, she recounted her entrance into Society under Lady Helen's patronage, blushed over Lord Camfield's
misinterpreted courtship, skipped over the
Belmont rout altogether, curiously enough,
and finally described her harrowing encounter with Mrs. Jennings.

"My dear child," said Lady Tabor,
deeply moved, "I only wish I had known! I

could have told you who your father was the moment I first set eyes on you."

"You knew?" Sir Aubrey and his bride spoke almost as one.

"All of Brighton knows — at least all of those old enough to remember the royal dukes in their youth. You have much the look of the royal family about you, my dear. I realize that hardly seems a compliment these days, but they were all very handsome as young men. Depend upon it, many people saw the resemblance. I daresay that is why Camfield courted you so assiduously. Certainly it is why you were taken to Society's bosom with so few questions asked."

"But I thought — Lady Helen —" Polly stammered.

"To be sure, Lady Helen is much admired, and rightfully so," concurred Lady Tabor, "but her patronage alone is not enough to make up for a lack of pedigree, and to be perfectly blunt, her stock has fallen considerably since her marriage."

"And 'ere I was feeling sadly neglected, me lady," put in Mr. Brundy. "You've made me feel right at 'ome, you 'ave."

"You flatter yourself," Lady Tabor assured him. "No weaver was *ever* at home at Inglewood. You are welcome to stay the night, but then we shall require a favor of you, Mr. Brundy. When you return to Brighton, I wonder if you would be good enough to send a notice to the newspapers announcing the engagement of Miss Crump to Sir Aubrey Tabor, along with the information that the pair, in company with Lady Tabor, the Marquess of Inglewood, and Viscount Sutcliffe, have removed to Inglewood, where the wedding will take place."

"But Mama, the wedding has already taken place," pointed out Sir Aubrey.

"A hole-and-corner affair at Gretna Green!" said her ladyship with a snort of derision. "No, Aubrey, you are going to post the banns and marry in church, like Christians! Polly will want some time to purchase her bride-clothes, and I daresay you will insist upon having Mr. Brundy to stand up with you, if Lady Helen is up to travelling in her condition —"

"What condition?" asked Mr. Brundy, galvanized to attention.

"Post the banns?" echoed Sir Aubrey. "But Mama, that would take three weeks!"

"Then I suppose you had best see the vicar as soon as possible," replied the dowager.

"What condition?" asked Mr. Brundy again.

"Oh, no, I will not!" insisted Sir Aubrey. "In three weeks' time, I intend to be firmly ensconced at Tabor Hall with my wife!"

"If your mama wishes you to be married at Inglewood, Aubrey, then I will not marry you anywhere else," Polly informed him.

"You are already married to me, my girl, and I intend to make very sure you don't forget it!" retorted Sir Aubrey.

"Oh, no you will not!" his mother interrupted, sparing Polly's blushes. "A fine thing it would look if your heir were to come along eight months after the ceremony!"

"But, Mama, we are legally wed!"

"If you care anything for your wife's reputation, Aubrey, you will not want the news of her elopement to reach the ears of the *ton*. Therefore, you will conduct yourselves as a betrothed couple until the banns are read."

"*What condition?*" demanded Mr. Brundy in a voice that would not be ignored.

"Lady Helen was a bit out of sorts on the morning of my departure, but I am sure she is quite all right," Lady Tabor assured him, having recollected a bit too late that Mr. Brundy was not yet aware of his wife's interesting malady. "Still, I have no doubt you are eager to get back to her."

"Aye, that I am," he agreed. "So much so that I think I'll decline your offer of 'ospitality. If I set out at once, I should be able to cover fifty miles before sundown."

A short time later, he took his leave, having been fortified with his first full meal in three days. In his pockets were sufficient funds to redeem Sir Aubrey's signet ring, watch, fob, and cravat-pin; in his ears, Lady Tabor's instructions for having the nuptial pair's belongings sent to Inglewood. Having delivered herself of these, Lady Tabor had borne Polly off to settle her in one of the guest bedchambers — one, Sir Aubrey noted ruefully, which would require that he tiptoe past his mother's room like a green youth trysting with a chambermaid, should he dare to attempt a midnight visit to his wife. Deprived of his bride, at least for the nonce, he walked with Mr. Brundy as far as the front stoop.

"I'll say this for you, Aubrey, you don't do a thing 'alfway," said Mr. Brundy. "When I asked you to get 'er out of me 'ouse, I never expected you to take 'er into your own."

"What are friends for?" asked Sir Aubrey with a modest shrug. "Having seen me married over the anvil, so to speak, would you find it redundant to stand up with me in church?"

"I wouldn't miss it," Mr. Brundy assured him.

"And I daresay Polly will want Lady Helen to attend her, so buy her a new bonnet or something, if you can spare a guinea or two."

Mr. Brundy nodded. "I think I can manage. You might do the same for your mum, you know. You were afraid she'd go off in an apoplexy, but it looks like she's taken your wife to 'er bosom."

"Which is more than I'll be allowed to do over the next three weeks, if Mama has anything to say to the matter," added Sir Aubrey with a grimace. "Ethan, since there are no words to thank you for your part in all this, I won't insult you by making the attempt. Nor will I detain you any longer, knowing — believe me, I know now! — how eager you are to get back to Lady Helen. I ask only that at some point over the next three weeks, while you are honeymooning with Lady Helen in blissful solitude, you will think of me with pity."

Mr. Brundy grinned and shook his head. "Sorry, Aubrey, but I'm going to be too busy," he said, and loped down the steps to the waiting carriage.

# Epilogue

Absence makes the heart grow fonder.
SEXTUS PROPERTIUS, *Elegies*

In a lamplit drawing room on the Marine Parade, Lady Helen sat alone before an inlaid card table solving a complicated Patience — a misnomer if ever there was one, she reflected restlessly. Her husband had been gone for more than a se'ennight, and during that time she'd had no word of his whereabouts, nothing at all since the night he had kissed her goodbye and set out with Sir Aubrey in search of Miss Crump. Her only consolation was that, if he were truly lying dead in a ditch, she should have received word of it long ere now.

The clock over the mantle chimed midnight, and Lady Helen sighed. Was this the other side of being in love, this feeling of being not quite whole unless the loved one were there? Another day was over, another day in which he had not come home. Perhaps tomorrow would be the one. In the meantime, she had the baby's well-being to think of, as well as her own. She stacked up the cards and was about to replace them in the box when a slight sound near the door caught her attention. She looked up and saw her husband leaning wearily against the doorframe.

"Ethan!" She leaped to her feet, knocking over the card table and scattering the cards she had just stacked. She crossed the room in scant seconds, and threw herself into Mr. Brundy's open arms.

"Ethan, I've missed you so! Did you find Polly? Is she married? Good heavens, you look dreadful!"

Except, of course, that he did not. To be sure, his clothing was certainly the worse for wear, and his chin bore a week's growth of beard, but the result was a certain rakish air that was not without appeal. Looking at him, she felt a stirring deep inside, one that had nothing to do with the child — his child — growing in her womb.

"I've missed you, too, 'elen, and yes, we found Polly, yes, she's married, and you're 'ardly in prime twig yourself." This last was delivered in a slightly accusatory tone, and he took her chin in his hand and tipped it up, surveying with displeasure her pale face and shadowed eyes. "Lady Tabor tells me you've been ill."

"Only in the mornings, darling, and it

soon passes," she assured him. "But tell me everything! Polly is married, then? How is Sir Aubrey taking it?"

In spite of his avowed refusal, Mr. Brundy thought of his friend's three-week delay and pitied him. " 'e's bearing up about as well as can be expected."

"Oh, dear! And I had hoped — Ethan, do you think she will be happy as a viscountess?"

He shook his head. "Not a chance, love. She'll 'ave to settle for being Lady Tabor of Tabor Hall."

Lady Helen's green eyes flew open wide, as her husband had known they would. "But you said she was married!"

"And so she is — to Aubrey. They were married over the anvil at Gretna Green four days ago. I witnessed the ceremony meself."

"Oh, I wish I might have seen it!"

"You can, if you like. Scottish law is not good enough for Sir Aubrey's mum. She insists they do it up proper in church, and no 'anky-panky until the knot is publicly tied." Mr. Brundy's smile turned wicked. "Is it just me, love, or is there something especially fitting about that?"

"I believe 'poetic justice' is the term you want."

"Aye, that or 'I told you so,' " he could not resist adding. "I knew all along that girl wasn't me sister."

"You were right, and I admit it," Lady Helen said magnanimously. "Still, considering how things have turned out, I don't regret taking her in."

"Nor do I, now that she's gone," replied Mr. Brundy generously. "They're all gone, love. At last, it's just you and me."

"But?"

"But what?" asked Mr. Brundy, all at sea.

"When a woman has been married as long as I have, she knows when something is troubling her husband," pronounced Lady Helen with all the wisdom of a bride of three months. "What is the matter, Ethan?"

"Oh, it's foolish, really," he said evasively, crossing the room to stand before the fireplace and stare into the dying flames.

"No, it isn't. Tell me."

He was silent for a long moment, during which Lady Helen wondered if he intended to answer at all. "It's 'ard to explain," he said at last. "I suppose all the mystery surrounding Miss Crump's father makes me wish I knew more about me own. I don't even know 'is name."

Lady Helen shook her head. "I'm sorry to disappoint you, darling, but you look nothing like any of the royal dukes — for which I am profoundly thankful."

A smile tugged at the corner of his mouth, but he continued to gaze unseeing into the flames. Lady Helen moved behind him, wrapping her arms about his waist and resting her head on his broad back.

"You have a name, Ethan," she said seriously. "It may not be the one you were born with, but you've made it into one your son will be proud to bear."

" 'elen, I know the 'ouse 'as been a bit crowded of late, but in case you've forgotten, I don't 'ave a son," pointed out Mr. Brundy.

"You may be right," admitted Lady Helen, much struck. "It might be a girl."

He stiffened in her embrace, and then turned to stare at her, eyes bulging and mouth agape.

Lady Helen smiled. "If it is a name you want, Mr. Brundy, what do you think of 'Papa'?"

He spread tentative fingers over her still-flat abdomen. " 'elen? Are you sure?"

She nodded. "Lady Tabor seemed quite certain, and as she has had five children of her own, I should think she would know, wouldn't you?"

"But — but 'ow'd *that* 'appen? We've 'ardly 'ad a minute alone!"

Lady Helen reached for the end of his cravat and pulled until the knot gave. "If you don't remember, Mr. Brundy, I wonder if it would be worth the effort to remind you."

Recognizing his cue, Mr. Brundy took her in his arms and applied himself to the task of demonstrating to his wife just how good his memory really was.

# Author's Note

Polly Hampton/Crump/Tabor, under all her various aliases, is a fictional character, as are all the other characters, both major and minor, with two notable exceptions: the Prince Regent and his brother, the Duke of Clarence. About this last, a word of explanation, if not apology, is perhaps called for. Since the Duke of Clarence (later King William IV) is known to have fathered at least eleven illegitimate children, ten of them by the comedienne Dorothea Jordan, I trust the reader will pardon my presumption in presenting him with one more.

# About the Author

Sheri Cobb South is the author of five popular young adult novels, as well as a number of short stories in various genres including mystery, young adult, and inspirational. Her first love has always been the Regency, however, and in 1999 she made her Regency debut with the publication of the critically acclaimed *The Weaver Takes a Wife*. She is currently working on the third and final book in the "Weaver" trilogy, *French Leave*, which is scheduled for publication in autumn of 2001.

Sheri lives near Mobile, Alabama with her husband and two children. You may send her e-mail at Cobbsouth@aol.com, or write to her c/o PrinnyWorld Press, P. O. Box 248, Saraland, AL 36571.

The employees of Thorndike Press hope you have enjoyed this Large Print book. All our Large Print titles are designed for easy reading, and all our books are made to last. Other Thorndike Press Large Print books are available at your library, through selected bookstores, or directly from us.

For information about titles, please call:

(800) 223-1244

or visit our Web site at:

www.gale.com/thorndike

To share your comments, please write:

Publisher
Thorndike Press
295 Kennedy Memorial Drive
Waterville, ME 04901